ONE CLASSY COWGIRL

THE QUEENS OF MONTANA, BOOK 2

VANESSA GRAY BARTAL

DRY CREEK PRESS

PROLOGUE

It was the wild stallion that did it.

The day began like any other. Dobbie sat in his saddle and watched endless herds of cattle stroll by him, like he had every day of his life. And then he saw it. Perched on a rock overlooking their progress was a lone, wild stallion.

"What's his story?" he asked Jeff, the other cowhand who was riding with him.

"He left his herd for some reason, and now they won't take him back," Jeff said.

Dobbie looked at the horse again, and something about its aloof expression made his chest tighten. He knew how the animal felt. He was twenty, alone, and miserable. He had been a part of a family once, but his wounded pride had made him throw it all away. What if they didn't accept him when he returned?

He shifted uncomfortably in the saddle. Pain and pride had made him run, but they quickly fled and left him stewing in his loneliness. The ache in his chest grew until it could no longer be ignored. Why had he left? Why had he stayed away so long?

Memories and feelings he had blocked for almost two years flooded his head and heart and temporarily blurred his vision. *I have to get out of here. I have to go home.* The words repeated over and over in his mind until they became a chant. He would wait until the end of the day, but no longer. Despite the fact that he would be leaving his employer in the lurch, he had to go as soon as possible.

Now that his mind was made up he was so anxious to leave sleep would be impossible. As soon as he returned to the bunkhouse after work, he packed his few belongings, walked to the nearest town to catch a bus, and then hopped a train. The many hours of travel gave him time to reflect on the past two years of his life. What did he have to show for them? A few memories and nothing more. He still had no belongings, except what fit into one small bag. Meanwhile, he had left a family behind who probably (hopefully) missed him.

He smiled to himself as he thought of the Chapmans. They were as much a part of him as his own parents had been, maybe more, because they took him in by choice. There was Matt, of course, the father and head of the family. Little Maggie was the youngest. He wondered if the intervening years had pulled her out of her girlish ways. He hoped not. Kitty would be sixteen now. When he left her, she was going through an awkward stage with glasses and braces. Those would most likely be gone, and he guessed she would be a beauty when her transformation was complete. And then there was Elizabeth. Libby. His smile widened, and he chuckled as he thought of some of their heated exchanges. Libby was a sweet sixteen-year-old last time he saw her. The vision of her standing in the kitchen in one of her pretty dresses was so clear, he felt like he could reach out and touch her. Of course she reserved her sweetness for everyone else. She had once thrown an iron skillet at him, and when it barely missed him, she haughtily told him she had purposed to miss.

"If I wanted to hit you, I would have." She had stood with her hands on her hips while she spoke. Then she had raised her head, turned her back, and stormed into the house.

He closed his eyes and rested his head on the window. The time to go home was past due; he had been away much too long, he thought, and then he fell asleep.

CHAPTER 1

Seventeen-year-old Libby Chapman surveyed her work with satisfaction. In the last few days, she had singlehandedly canned over two hundred pints of jam, and she was already mentally calculating the money they would bring in. One jar in particular was so pretty she contemplated entering it in the county fair and then quickly dismissed the idea. She would rather have money than praise.

The opening of the front door startled her out of her reverie, and she cleared the counter to start on another batch.

"Maggie, you'd better take those shoes off," she called in the direction of the door. Her youngest sister, Maggie, was fourteen and still acted like a ten-year-old boy. She was in charge of picking all the berries for the jam. It was a hot, sweaty, and itchy job for which Libby had offered to pay her, but Maggie refused the money. There was nothing she liked better than working outside and getting dirty, something which the fastidiously clean Libby would never understand.

"It's not Maggie, but I did take my boots off," a male voice said, and Libby spun to look at him.

"Dobbie," she breathed. Then she dropped her dishtowel and burst into tears.

For a moment he looked at her in open-mouthed surprise, and then he came forward and gathered her gently into his arms. She bunched the front of his shirt in her hands and sobbed into it while he tried to orient his senses. A crying Libby was the last thing he expected. She was far more likely to throw a frying pan at his head. He had prepared himself for her anger, but not for her sadness.

"Hey," he said, easing his hand soothingly over her hair. "What's this about?"

"You didn't say goodbye," she said. Even though the sound was muffled, he could hear the familiar angry edge in her tone, and it made him smile.

"I would have, if I knew you would miss me this much."

"I didn't miss you at all," she lied and clutched his shirt tighter. In truth, she had missed him horribly every day of the two years he had been absent, and she was so surprised over that fact, she refused to think about it. But now he was here, and all her sadness over his sudden departure came up to hit her in the face. She let go his shirt and rested her cheek on his chest before sliding her arms around his waist. He had never held her before; strange it should feel so comfortable. His strong and steady heartbeat was a reassuring reality of his presence, and her tears began to fall again, gently this time.

They stood frozen in time with their arms around each other, each wrapped in his or her own thoughts of how odd, yet perfect, the moment was. He caught her scent and closed his eyes. Nothing smelled as good as Libby. She smelled like home and every good thing home meant. Libby closed her eyes, too, but her thoughts were too jumbled to be coherent. All she knew was Dobbie was here, standing in her kitchen, and she had missed him more than she would ever admit to anyone.

Dobbie eased his hand to her face and tipped it up. He used his thumb to wipe her tears. "This won't do, Lib. With our history people are going to think I punched you and made you cry." It was true; they had never gotten along in all the years they had known each other. They had bickered endlessly, and at times she actually had thrown pots and pans at him or chased him with her broom.

Libby used the opportunity to study his face and observe all the changes. He was all grown up, and there were new lines of maturity where boyishness had once been. Where had he gone? What had he been doing? What other difference had time wrought in him? "You're twenty now," she said. She lightly traced her fingers over his face and tried to memorize everything that was different. Two years apart had aged him into a man, and she mourned the transition, mourned the fact that she hadn't been able to bear witness.

"And you're almost eighteen." He plucked a stray lock of hair off her wet cheek and tucked it behind her ear.

In all the time she had known him, he had never once forgotten her birthday. Even when they were in the midst of a steaming row he would call a truce long enough to give her a card or present. Two years ago he bought her a beautiful teapot, and it remained as one of her most treasured possessions. Last year he sent her a card with no return address, and she had stared at it for days wondering where he was, hoping he would come home.

"Why did you come back?" she asked. She knew why he went away. The girl he had spoken for, her older sister Anne, fell in love with someone else and went back east to attend college with him. A heartbroken Dobbie had left soon after, never to be heard from again —until today.

"I heard you need a foreman." His hands settled easily on her waist, fingers clasped behind her back. Had her waist always been so small? He couldn't remember.

Some part of her brain acknowledged the fact that they were still embracing, but she didn't move away. Instead she shifted her position and settled more firmly in his grasp, sliding her hands up to rest behind his neck. "We needed a foreman two years ago," she said, and she couldn't keep the accusation out of her tone. Anne had been their ranch's foreman, with Dobbie next in line. When Anne and Dobbie both went away, her father had been left in the lurch. He hired the first person he could find, an unskilled and dishonest man who nearly ran the ranch into the ground.

Dobbie's hands tightened on her waist. "I couldn't stay, you know that."

She tensed. "I know no such thing. A lot of people were counting on you, and a lot of people were hurt when you went away. Maggie cried for days." That wasn't exactly true. Maggie had been upset, to be sure, but it was Libby who did the crying and Maggie who did the brunt of the comforting.

Now he was scowling. "I should have known you would take Anne's side, despite how much she hurt me. I guess it's true what they say about apples staying close to their trees. How many men have *you* jilted since I went away?"

She struggled to get out of his embrace, but he pinned her to his chest. His arms were like a vise, but she still managed to turn herself around so she was trapped with her back to his front. When Maggie entered the room a minute later, she saw Dobbie trying hard to clamp down on his amusement while Libby slithered like an electric eel, trying to break free from his hold.

"Were you two kissing?" Maggie asked. She set a basket of berries on the counter and studied Dobbie and Libby with a quizzical expression.

Dobbie chortled, and the sound sent Libby over the edge. She stomped on his foot and moved out of his grasp when he bent to massage his throbbing toes.

"I would sooner kiss a rattlesnake," Libby yelled as she turned and stalked from the room.

"You'd have an easier time getting the snake to pucker up," Dobbie called after her. "And *that* is why I never take my boots off in the house!"

CHAPTER 2

*L*ibby waited to reemerge from her room until she was sure Dobbie was gone. Maggie was still in the kitchen sorting berries. Libby put a cookie on a plate and set it on the table in front of her baby sister.

"So, Dobbie's back," Maggie said happily, picking up the cookie with berry-stained fingers and breaking it in half.

"Dobbie's back," Libby echoed without the happy inflection. She set about making her next batch of jam. Maggie, bless her, had already picked over and washed everything, so Libby had only to put them in the large pot and add the remaining ingredients.

"Where do you think he was all this time?" Maggie asked, licking melted chocolate off her doubly messy fingers.

Libby paused in her preparations. She had spent many nights wondering that same thing. "I don't know."

Dobbie had no family besides them. He had been their next-door neighbor until he was fourteen, when his parents died in a house fire he miraculously escaped. Her father took him in as part of their family and also as a ranch hand. From the beginning, he and Anne had been pushed together, although no one said anything out loud. They were the same age, had similar interests, and it was assumed they would get married and run the ranch together. Only Anne hadn't loved Dobbie. She loved Will, and her abandonment broke Dobbie's heart. Despite his bluster Dobbie had a soft heart, and it killed Libby to think how her sister's rejection must have wounded him. Just as it had pained her so many nights when she imagined him alone and lonely, somewhere far away. Many nights she had fallen asleep murmuring vague prayers for him and hoping he was all right. She wasn't sure why his pain should bother her so, maybe because it was her sister who did the hurting, or maybe because Dobbie was like family to her. She couldn't remember ever not knowing him.

She set the jam to boil and finished her supper preparations. It was all so automatic for her now she barely had to think about it. Her mother had died when she was ten years old, and almost immediately Libby took up the household duties. Twelve year old Anne had been busy helping run the ranch. Eight-year-old Kitty and six year old Maggie were too little to do much of anything. Libby didn't mind, though. She loved cooking, cleaning, baking, sewing, quilting, and everything else that went along with homemaking, and she did it with flair, if she did say so herself. Over the years she had gained a reputation in the community as an elegant lady, and it was something she was proud of. She wore a pretty dress every day, and always had perfect hair and makeup. She was a control freak when it came to the cleanliness of the house and the quality of the food, but they were a reflection of her and therefore had to be perfect.

Despite her love of domesticity, she had no plans to settle down and be someone's wife, and least of all did she plan to do it here in the backcountry of Montana. No, she wanted to go to the city like Anne and get a degree in business or design. Then she wanted to own a company and make a million dollars. People thought her interests revolved around food, cleaning products, and yarn, but they were wrong. Her interests were purely mercenary, and she was going to get out of this uncultured wasteland if it killed her.

By the time she canned the last batch of jam and set supper on the table, she had all but forgotten her irritation with Dobbie, but that was their way. They blew up at each other frequently, but then it was easily and quickly forgotten.

When he arrived for supper, dusty and exhausted, he also seemed to have abandoned their quarrel.

"Libby, I had almost forgotten how good your food smells and looks," he said when he took in the sight of the table. "I can't wait to remember how it tastes."

Libby put her hands on her hips. "Don't you dare sit down, you filthy cowboy." He was covered head to toe in grime.

"Lib, I'm too tired and too hungry to take a shower."

He did look famished and exhausted, and she softened somewhat. "At least wash your hands."

"I did." He held out his hands for her inspection.

"Did you use mud for soap? Come here." She took him by the hand and led him to the kitchen sink. "Here, I bought this off the Internet. It's for auto mechanics, so I figure it should work for cowhands, too. Don't forget to scrub your nails." She turned to go, but he stopped her.

"Show me how." He gave her a mischievous smile. When they were younger she used to admonish him for not cleaning his room properly, and he would feign ignorance in order to get her to do it for him.

She suppressed the smile that tugged at her lips and bent to retrieve a nailbrush. She kept it on hand because all of the cowboys who entered the kitchen were always filthy, and they all knew how she felt about dirty hands.

She lathered Dobbie's hands and started to scrub his nails, and that's when it happened. A tight stinging sensation started in the pit of her stomach, sort of like a lit firework uncoiling. She dropped the brush and looked at Dobbie in alarm. Her alarm grew when she saw a matching expression on his face. He was studying her with a strange sort of intensity, and when their eyes met, he didn't look away or blink.

His thumbs caressed the backs of her hands, and she drew in a shaky breath.

"Are you done?" Maggie asked. "We're starving."

Libby dropped her gaze and quickly finished scrubbing Dobbie's nails, which was no easy task because her hands were now shaking. "There," she said in a breathless voice that didn't resemble her own.

"Thank you," Dobbie said in his usual steady way, and her heart picked up its pace.

She kept her eyes downcast as she sat at the table and after the prayer, too. What was that? What was happening to her? This was Dobbie, the guy she couldn't stand and loved like family, all rolled into one. He was a rough and tumble cowboy with a high school education. He bore zero resemblance to the sophisticated and cultured man of her dreams.

"I guess I've been gone too long because the place is unrecognizable to me," Dobbie said, loading his fork with an impossible amount of roast beef. "I could almost swear I saw some goats out there, but that can't be. Cows and goats don't belong together."

Libby glanced up sharply. "You leave my goats alone."

"Oh, brother. I should have guessed they were yours. No one else is brainless enough to raise goats around here. I sure hope they don't meet with any unfortunate accidents." He stuffed another bite of beef in his mouth and wagged his brows at her.

"If anything happens to my goats, you'll be sorry, Dobbie."

"Oh, really, Libby? And what are you going to do to me?" The way he said it and raised one eyebrow made her tingle all over and glance away.

She took a breath and forced herself to look back at him. "I'll starch your underpants and never bake you an apple pie again."

His mouth puckered into a pout. "I didn't know you could play so unfair, Libby."

"After two years away, you really don't know me at all, do you, Dobbie?" she asked, and that thought kept him quiet for the rest of supper.

When the meal was finished, everyone vacated the kitchen except Libby. She stood to clear the table.

"Don't you get tired of it?" Dobbie asked. She thought he left with everyone else, but now she looked up to see him lounging in the doorway.

"What?"

"Doing all the cooking and cleaning and never getting a break. I mean, you're seventeen. You should be out with friends. Or your boyfriend."

Was it her imagination or was there a strange inflection on the last word? "From what I remember, you didn't go out much when you were my age."

He smiled. "You make me sound so old. And besides, my girlfriend lived twenty feet away." He had resumed his place in the bunkhouse with the other ranch hands as if he never went away.

"How do you know my boyfriend doesn't?" she asked, and enjoyed watching his momentary scowl.

"Because I'm the youngest hand," he said, satisfied with his logic.

"Can't you picture me with an older man?"

He scanned her up and down. He *could* picture her with an older man. She had always been mature for her age, and she liked things from another time, like the dress she was wearing now. It looked like something from the Kennedy era. "Are you dating one of the hands?" he demanded, and then hastened to add, "I like to keep on top of what my men are up to."

"No, I am not dating one of the hands. I've had enough of cowboys to last a lifetime," she said. Something about her tone gave him pause. Or maybe it was the little shudder she added at the end.

"Did something happen?" He mentally reviewed the other ranch hands. If they had done something to her, they would be lucky to see another sunrise.

"Didn't Dad tell you why he let the foreman go?" she asked, as she busied herself at the sink, avoiding his eyes.

"He said it was because he was incompetent."

"He edited some of the details."

Dobbie clenched his hands into tight fists, straightened, and took a step forward. "What did he do to you?" His tone was like ice. The instantaneous fury caused a buzzing noise in his ears. He swallowed it down so he could hear what she had to say.

"Made me uncomfortable, mostly. It was subtle in the beginning, the dropping by the house in the middle of the day, the inappropriate comments followed by unconvincing apologies. He scared me, but I didn't know why, so I tried to keep Maggie or Kitty in the house with me, but then a couple of weeks ago," she broke off and tried to steady her quaking hands.

Dobbie strode over and stood stiffly beside her. "A couple of weeks ago, what?"

"I was alone in the kitchen and he," she stopped and swallowed hard, shaking her head. "I don't want to talk about it."

"I'll hear it from someone eventually. It might as well be you."

He was right. There were few secrets on the ranch. She took a breath and tried to say it calmly and without emotion as she stared at the sink, watching the bubbles pop listlessly. "He pinned me to the wall and touched me. I tried to get away, but couldn't. Maggie came in and started screaming hysterically."

Dobbie stared at her, horrified, unable to take in what she was saying. That someone would touch Libby in that way was... He couldn't even find words for his volcanic emotions. He eased the dish out of her hand and turned her to face him. He rested his hands on her shoulders and peered earnestly into her eyes. "Libby, he could have...And Maggie is so small and helpless." His eyes squeezed together, and he had to fight a wave of nausea. His girls, his family, alone and unprotected while some man laid hands on Libby.

"But Kitty's not. She heard Maggie scream and brought one of Dad's guns. She cocked it and told him to get out. I think she would have used it, too."

Dobbie tried to picture quiet and studious Kitty holding a gun on a grown man. It was difficult, but it was unwise to underestimate the Chapman sisters. "I'm sorry," he said sincerely.

Libby knew it was more than an I'm-sorry-for-what-happened-to-you apology. "Why are you sorry? It's not your fault."

"Yes, it is. If I had been here it wouldn't have happened."

She read the guilt and pain in his eyes and knew he meant it. "Dobbie," she said gently. "It wasn't your fault. Even if you had been here something like that might have happened. You can't blame your-self for someone else's bad actions."

He still looked unconvinced and stared at her as if he now owed her something. She didn't understand it, and she didn't like the way it made her feel—like she was his responsibility. They were family by circumstance, and nothing more. She had to be clear on that.

He didn't give her the opportunity because he abruptly let her go and picked up the dishtowel. "Your water's getting cold," he said, and she slowly resumed washing while he dried, another first. For as long as she had known him, Dobbie had never once volunteered to do the dishes. He was more likely to label it as women's work and tend to the horses outside, which had always suited Libby fine.

She didn't like the new order of things one little bit, and she tossed about for a subject that would get them back on familiar footing. "How bad is the ranch?" she asked. Her father might try to sugarcoat it, but Dobbie wouldn't.

"Bad. If we have a bad summer, we might not make it."

Shock kept her silent. Might not make it? Could they really lose the ranch? No, it wasn't possible; she couldn't bear it. It wasn't the life for her, but her father loved it, and Maggie, and Dobbie. Despite his two-year absence, she knew he felt like the ranch was a part of him.

"Isn't there anything we can do?" she asked.

"I have a few ideas, but it's going to take some convincing."

"He'll come around. Dad trusts you," she said.

"Do you? It's going to involve everyone if it goes through."

She thought about that. Did she trust Dobbie? Besides her father, she couldn't think of anyone she trusted more, except…

"Will you go away again?"

She didn't realize her voice sounded small and uncertain and hurt, but Dobbie did, and the sound made him wince. If he had known his leaving would hurt her, he never would have gone. Why had he left? And why had he stayed away?

"This is my home, Lib. You are my family," he said.

"We always were," she said.

"Sometimes it takes going away to figure things out."

"That wasn't a no," she said with some of her old fire.

He suppressed a smile and laid his hand on hers. "I promise you this: I won't leave as long as I'm welcome here."

She couldn't imagine a scenario where Dobbie would ever be unwelcome. He was as much a part of them as their home and their land. "Do you really promise, Dobbie?" she asked in the same vulnerable voice that melted his heart. She gazed up at him, so trusting, so open, he thought his heart might burst free from his chest and gallop away to escape the pain of it.

"I promise, Elizabeth," he said in the new gentle tone, and they finished the dishes in silence.

CHAPTER 3

The next morning Dobbie woke early. Libby was always the first one up, and he wanted to see her before his day began. There was no reason why; he didn't need to tell her anything. He simply wanted to be with her a few minutes, and he tried not to delve too deeply into his motives.

He stood in the shadow of the doorway unnoticed while she bustled around preparing breakfast for the family. She was a sight for sore eyes. He had no idea how she managed to look so pretty and put together before the sun was up, but somehow she did. Her white dress was spotless and would remain that way, no matter what she did with her day. Maybe mud refused to land on her. Or maybe when it did she ordered it away and it obeyed. Either way, she was always immaculate. He had the almost overwhelming desire to close the gap between them and take her in his arms again, to pick her up, swing her around, and then…and then what?

"Did you know you hum first thing in the morning?" he asked.

She startled and whirled to face him, a smile on her lips. "I do? Must be because this is my favorite time of day. It's so peaceful."

"Want me to go away and leave you alone?" His tone was teasing, but he dreaded the answer might be yes.

"Don't be silly," she said. As she watched him cross the room and pour himself a mug of coffee, she was surprised by how much she meant it. She always rose before anyone else, and she coveted her few minutes of alone time before the rest of the family awoke. But she didn't mind having Dobbie there. In fact, she rather enjoyed the sight of him. She busied herself at the coffee pot pouring her own mug so he wouldn't read any of her startling thoughts in her expression.

They sat at the table sipping their coffee in silence; each one was trying hard not to think about the other and failing miserably. Dobbie had missed moments like these, moments of utter peace and contentment, of security and wholeness. Over the last couple of years, a few of the places he'd stayed at had been friendly. But none of them had felt like home. The Chapmans, though not his family by birth, were his family by choice. Being with them again on the ranch he loved filled a void in his heart he hadn't realized he possessed until he left home two years ago. Now that he was back, he had no desire to ever leave again.

Libby noticed his cup was empty and stood to fill it. He grabbed her hand and held her back. "Lib, sit down. Don't fuss over me."

She shook him off, filled his cup, and sat. "Someone needs to, Dobbie. Who looked after you while you were gone?"

"No one," he said.

She frowned into her cup. She had never been able to stand the thought of him in pain or alone, hurting with no one to care for him, no one to feed him, no one to try and wash the stains out of his denim or do any of the other million things she had tried to do for him over the years.

He took one of her hands and clasped it, giving it a soft squeeze. "No one does it as well as you, no one ever has." Even when they bickered, she had never failed to make sure his laundry was done and he was well fed. She didn't have to feed or clothe him—he could have eaten with the other cowhands. But since he first moved from the main house to the bunkhouse, she wouldn't let him escape family meals. And if he forgot to bring his laundry to her, she would go into the bunkhouse to retrieve it and then place it neatly in his drawers when it was finished, folded and fresh smelling. Was it any wonder the smell of laundry powder reminded him of her? Her pampering treatment was one more thing he hadn't realized was vital to him until he was suddenly without it. For the first few months after he went away, he kept expecting to hear her voice chiding him to eat properly or brush the dust off his chaps.

They sat in comfortable silence once more, sipping their coffee, unaware they were still clasping hands. If either of them had thought about it, they would have realized how different their new relationship was from their old one. Before, the only time they had touched was when she was whacking him with a broom. Or when he was trying to pin her arms to keep her from hitting him. Now every once in a while their eyes caught and held, and they smiled, a tremor of warm affection bouncing between them.

Not until they heard her father stirring in the next room did they realize how intimate and cozy the kitchen felt. They both glanced at their still-clasped hands before guiltily jerking apart. Libby hopped to her feet and bustled around, preparing her father's breakfast. They breathed a combined sigh of relief when he entered the kitchen and found nothing amiss between them. Each thought maybe it had been his or her imagination that had made things feel so *right* between them. Neither realized that, while having these thoughts, they were staring at each other over the kitchen table.

For the next few days Dobbie and Libby settled into a peaceful routine. He started work before sunup, meaning they didn't see each other until supper at night. But after supper was finished, he stayed to help her with the dishes, and they talked, really talked, for the first time in their lives. For Libby it helped to ease some of the loneliness she'd felt since Anne went away. The ranch was remote, and she had only her sisters for company, but Kitty usually had her head stuck in a book, and Maggie was too young to confide in. Anne had been Libby's best friend, and she missed her greatly. She wondered if Dobbie was using her to ease his ache over the loss of Anne, and the thought hurt somehow.

It was the longest period of peace that had ever existed between them, so of course it had to come to an end. Early one morning Libby was out milking her goat when Dobbie wandered by. For some reason the sight of her looking so pretty and fresh and feminine grated on his nerves.

"You can't milk a goat in a dress, Libby," he snapped.

"Watch me," she said with equal passion.

He leaned against the fence and did exactly that. She was lovely, by far the most beautiful girl he'd ever seen. And after his travels, he'd seen a lot of girls. "Where did you learn to milk?"

"You learn what you have to, I guess."

It was a cynical thing for her to say, and it bothered him. She was seventeen years old; she shouldn't have to face anything that made her hard and cynical. "Why do you have these stupid things, anyway? They're useless." He kicked the post, irritable for reasons he couldn't articulate.

Her eyes flashed fire at him. "They are not useless." She gathered her bucket and breezed by him, but he caught her arm.

"Prove it," he said with a taunting smile that baffled her because of her reaction to it. For an instant she was immobilized, and then she wrenched her arm out of his grasp.

"I don't have to prove anything to you, Shane Dobbins."

He blinked at her in confusion a few times. "No one has used my real name in a long time."

The way he said it made a blush rise to her cheeks. Instead of answering, she raised her chin and walked away, trying not to stumble with her heavy bucket of milk.

Later that night there was a new dish at supper. Libby usually deferred to her father and Dobbie's preference for meat and potatoes, so when she went out on a limb and made something unusual, they indulged her without complaint. Still, Dobbie eyed the little round disks with suspicion before piling one on his plate. But when he tasted it, he opened his eyes in pleased surprise and added two more before the rest of the family could devour them.

"What are these little fried things?" Libby's father, Matt Chapman, asked.

"Goat cheese," Libby said and glared at Dobbie with a challenging glint in her eyes.

Clearly she had won this round, but he didn't mind. He made sure no one was looking, and then he winked at her and smiled. A pretty blush spread over her cheeks before she dropped her gaze to her plate, confused. Dobbie had made her feel a lot of things over the years, namely irritation. But never this flustered confusion. Libby was a girl who knew what she was about. This new lack of understanding confounded her in a most unpleasant way.

And so she avoided him. When it came time for their after dinner dish session, she detained her father with a question so he and Dobbie ended up talking about the ranch until the dishes were done. She avoided him in the early mornings when he tended to be near the barn, and she wouldn't meet his eyes over the supper table. All in all, he was confused, and he missed her like crazy, the sight of her, the smell of her, the sound of her voice. Most of all he missed the way he felt when he was with her, and the lack made him irritable.

Finally when he could stand it no more, he ambushed her one evening after supper. She crept to the barn to check her goats, but not before she looked around, probably making sure he was nowhere in sight. He saw it from his hiding place behind a bush, and his temper flared. How dare she hide from him as if he were some sort of stalker waiting to ambush her. He'd show her. While she was in the goat pen, he darted from his hiding place and saddled his horse. He was waiting for her when she finished. She started when she saw him and then tried to pretend she didn't.

"Oh, Dobbie, hello." She smoothed a hand over her perfectly coiffed hair, her tell that she was nervous and self-conscious.

"Take a ride with me," he said, and it wasn't a request.

She looked down to indicate her dress.

"Are you too good to ride side saddle, Miss Priss?" He knew he was being too hard on her, might possibly even be mean, but she was making him crazy, and he didn't know why.

She held up her hands in surrender, and he swooped to pick her up with one arm. He settled her in front of him sideways, and she had to cross her legs in order to squeeze into the small space. His right arm retained the reins and skimmed her back while his left arm settled on her waist to hold her steady. She rested her hands on his forearm for lack of a better place to put them and thought how ridiculously muscular they were. Her eyes followed the line of his arm up to his chest and shoulders. He was all muscle, and not the kind that came from the gym, but the kind that developed from riding a horse, pulling calves, and fixing fences. His gaze remained steadily on the horizon, allowing her to study his face undetected. His hair was sandy blond but always appeared darker because it was usually caked with grime after work. His eyes were swirls of brown and green. His nose had a notch in it from where a calf kicked his face. And his lips, well, his lips were his best feature. They were full and red and pretty, a descriptor he would not appreciate, if she ever used it on him. He was very handsome, and she wondered why she had never noticed it before. She didn't have to ponder long. As her sister's boyfriend, he had been off limits to her. But he was still off-limits, wasn't he? Just because he wasn't Anne's boyfriend anymore didn't mean he never had been. Wasn't it ten shades of wrong to consider the handsomeness of your sister's ex?

She would have fallen off the horse if she knew he was having similar thoughts about her. Anne was pretty with long brown hair, gold highlights, and big doe brown eyes. But she was rough and tumble and had usually been covered in as much dirt as he had. Libby was always clean, fresh, and feminine. And she smelled like strawberries, even in the winter. She was soft and vulnerable, and his arms tightened slightly with the need to protect her. Her hair was brown, but her highlights were auburn. Her brown eyes were smaller than Anne's, but her lashes were long and thick, and ever since he came home he found himself watching her, waiting for to blink so he could stare at her lashes.

"Why did you cut your hair?" he asked suddenly. "Last I remember it was down to here." He made a sawing motion in the middle of her back. Now it hung to her shoulders.

"It was too girlish. I wanted to look more grown up. Do you think I look more grown up?" She tipped her head and waited for his inspection.

He gave her an affectionate smile. "You'll always be a girl to me, I think."

She regained her position against his chest with a decided thump.

"A very *pretty* girl," he added softly, and squeezed her waist where his hand rested.

She smiled and then frowned again, in confusion this time, but so did he. This was Libby. Why was she affecting him this way? He cleared his throat and moved to a safer topic.

"I have something I need to talk to you about. I think we're going to have to take on some tourists this summer."

"Is it that bad?" her tone was the proper mix of shock and horror. Tourists, *ugh.*

"It's that bad," he said grimly. Many surrounding ranches had already taken on tourists to help pay the bills, but her family had always resisted, if for no other reason than pride. The thought of strangers invading their privacy was unpleasant, to say the least.

"Anyway, I'm going to need your help if it's going to work. I want it to be special, the way you make everything special. Plus, details aren't my strong suit, and it's going to require a lot of time on the Internet, time I don't have and can't afford to take. Will you do it?"

"Of course," she said. She almost felt excited as plans and menus ran around in her head. "Where will they stay?" They didn't have any guest accommodations, unless they cleared the cowboys out of the bunkhouse.

"They won't stay. It's going to be a wilderness adventure."

Some of her enthusiasm dimmed. Wilderness wasn't her forte. She had envisioned elegant gatherings at the ranch, not glorified camping.

"Relax," he said, and his thumb smoothed up and down her waist.

"I'll get Hank to do the cooking. He's been looking for some extra income."

Hank was a retired cowboy in town. He had lots of experience sleeping under the stars and cooking over an open fire.

"It's already June. How are you going to get people to come?"

"They're already coming," he said. "I advertised the first week I was here, and a group of ten is coming in three weeks."

"Three weeks," she exclaimed. "Do you know how much work that's going to take?" She bolted up to look at him again and almost toppled off the horse. He tightened his grip on her, and her hands slid up to grab his shirt.

"You can do it, Libby. If anyone can it's you. Why do you think I came to you?"

"Because there is no one else," she guessed.

"No, it's because I trust you. If you had an army at your disposal, I'm convinced you could take over the world."

She smiled and rested her head on his chest, ridiculously pleased by the statement. Dobbie wasn't one for handing out compliments lightly. Unbidden, her hand crept up until it rested gently on his chest. She smoothed her fingers over him a few times, an affectionate little gesture. He smelled like horses and leather and the outdoors, and she inhaled deeply. One of her favorite things about the ranch was the men. Not that she was boy crazy—the ranch was too isolated for that, but she liked how the men were all *men*. They were large and masculine, and they made her feel small and feminine in comparison. She enjoyed feeling cared for and protected. Her happy thoughts and the gentle swaying of the horse lulled her to sleep after a few minutes.

Dobbie felt Libby relax against him and knew she was asleep, and no wonder. She worked harder than any girl he had ever met, except Anne. She was always cooking, baking, cleaning, canning, working in her garden or with her infernal goats. Thoughts of her brought a temptation he was unable to suppress. He secured the horse's reigns around the saddle horn and wrapped both arms around her. The smell of strawberries overwhelmed him, and he closed his eyes and inhaled before brushing a light kiss on the top of her head. She stirred slightly and curled her arm around his waist. He froze. What was he doing? This was Libby, the little sister of the girl he had once thought he would marry. How could he be feeling what he was now feeling? And for that matter, what *was* he feeling? He could no longer deny he was attracted to her and had been since he stepped into her kitchen, but to what end? Anne's betrayal had left him heartbroken, and even if it hadn't, Libby wasn't for him. Besides the fact they couldn't seem to get along more than ten minutes, they were too different. He was a cowboy to the core and wanted nothing more than the life he had now. While she wanted, well, he wasn't sure what she wanted, but he was sure it wasn't him, at least not permanently.

She moved slightly, nestling further into his embrace, and her pretty lips parted in a sigh. All he would have to do was lean down a tiny bit and touch his lips to hers and… He shook his head to clear it. No. Being with her was a luxury he couldn't afford until he worked through his strange new reaction to her. He would have to put some distance between them, even though the thought made him sad. She was his only friend now, and he had started to look forward to their evenings together. He had missed her desperately the last few days, had felt empty without the after-supper talks he had come to look forward to.

Wait. *She* had been avoiding *him* lately. Was it for the same reason? Was she attracted to him and unsure of what to do about it? The thought was both thrilling and terrifying. It was one thing for him to fight this battle on his own, but if they were both feeling it, they might as well be doomed.

They reached the house, and he shook her slightly. "Libby, sweetheart." He bit his lip, wincing. Where did that come from?

She opened her eyes and blinked at him, long lashes fanning. "I fell asleep on a horse. Does that make me a real cowgirl?" She blinked sleepily up at him as she awaited his answer, her head still resting on his chest.

"Do you want to be a cowgirl?" It was a teasing question, but it was loaded. What did Libby want? And how was it possible he didn't know if she was the person he had once known best in the world?

She smiled sleepily but didn't answer.

Dobbie eased off the horse and put his arms up to lift her down. She slid down him and rested her hands on his chest, still blinking owlishly in sleep-addled confusion. He was reluctant to let her go, but he summoned his newfound vow to avoid her and took a step away.

"Thanks for the ride," he said. He tipped his hat, as he might have for any stranger, but the effect was ruined by his embarrassingly husky voice.

She continued to blink up at him, confused by his abrupt change in demeanor, still not all the way awake. The longer they stood there, the more tension crept between them. Finally when he could stand it no more, he lifted a shaking hand, gathered a wisp of hair, and smoothed it behind her ear.

"You should go inside, sweetheart."

Libby nodded, took a step away, tossed him one final perplexed look over her shoulder, and went into the house.

CHAPTER 4

Dobbie's resolve to distance himself lasted until exactly the next morning. Libby was watering her garden, and he stood back to watch. It was a large and beautiful garden, filled with flowers and vegetables and herbs of every sort. Except for the plowing in the spring, she, Kitty, and Maggie did all of it themselves. Then Libby spent weeks pickling, canning, and freezing all the produce to last throughout the year. Why had he never realized how talented she was or how hard she worked? Instead, he had purposely made more work for her by clomping his muddy boots on her clean floors. More than once she had actually chased and beaten him with a broom, and he smiled over the memories as he watched her.

He pressed his booted foot on the hose and waited to release it until she turned the hose on herself in order to look for a blockage. The water sprayed her face, and she glared at him like a wet furious cat, knowing immediately he was the cause. He smiled impishly at her until she directed the hose at him.

"How about a bath, cowboy?"

"Don't do it, Libby," he warned, but of course she did. She drenched him in the freezing well water while he advanced on her and wrangled the hose from her hands. Somehow in the process, she ended up in his arms pressed tightly to his chest. His dust was smearing on her immaculate dress, but she didn't squirm away in revulsion. Instead, she blinked up at him in the new way she had lately, as if he were a creature she had never seen before, one who required intense study. He wondered if he looked at her the same way, and if it had the same effect her unwavering gaze had on him.

"I've never seen you dirty before," he said.

"Funny, I've never seen you clean," she said and laughed when he nuzzled his grungy, dripping nose against her cheek. He placed a light kiss there, and she stopped laughing.

"We need to talk tonight," she said seriously, her hand toying with the top button of his shirt. He sobered but did nothing to ease her away from him. Why did girls have to talk so much? He wasn't ready to discuss what was happening between them when he didn't understand it himself.

"About what?" he asked nervously.

"Camping."

It was possibly the last thing he expected her to say, and his ready rebuffs died on his lips. "Camping?"

"Yes, camping. As in the camping trip I'm supposed to be planning. It's a logistical nightmare. I have no idea how I'm going to pull it off, and I need some more information from you." She gave his chest a little shove and sidestepped out of his embrace.

He was strangely disappointed, and a little bit annoyed. When he thought she wanted to talk about them, he panicked, and now that he knew she wanted to talk about camping, he was angry. "Let me get this straight: you want to talk about camping tonight. Camping is the thing you want to talk about. Tonight. *Camping.*"

She was looking at him like he was crazy, and maybe he was now. Maybe seeing Libby Chapman again had forced him to lose whatever was left of his sanity. He couldn't ever remember feeling so confused or irrational before.

"Yes, Dobbie, camping," she said with some of her usual temper she only reserved for him.

"Fine." He bit the word off and stormed away.

Of course he was penitent by the time supper arrived that night. It wasn't her fault a new and dangerous attraction simmered between them. She was as caught up in it as he was, and fighting it as hard. Probably harder, he thought with a frown. Knowing Libby, she wouldn't go down easy, wouldn't be willing to surrender her pride and admit what was happening between them.

His frown fled when he walked into the kitchen and recognized many of his favorite foods on the table. Libby stole a shy glance at him, and he smiled at her. For Libby, food was love. Preparing Dobbie's favorites was her way of apologizing for whatever had made him angry. Something deeper and more real than fleeting attraction settled over his heart and tried to take root, but he willed it away. He would not fall in love with this girl who already meant the world to him, not now, not ever. She was all wrong for him, totally and completely. He needed someone who… Who did he need, and how exactly would she be different from Libby? He concentrated so hard on that thought he was silent throughout dinner.

The meal finished and Libby's hand trembled slightly when she cleared his plate. He looked around and realized not only were they alone, but his stony silence was making her nervous. He caught her hand and brought it to his lips, placing a gentle kiss on her knuckles.

"Thank you for supper," he said sincerely. "It was delicious, as usual. You're the best cook I know, Libby girl." He wondered if he had ever complimented her on a meal before. By the surprise in her eyes, he guessed not. His thumb continued to skim over her knuckles. "If you make a habit of taking care of me I'm going to think you're nice deep down. Deep, deep down."

"I'm only doing my job; cooking, cleaning, and caring for the difficult animals." She smiled and touched the fingers of her free hand to the place where his nose was broken. They both remembered the day he broke it, the day the calf kicked him. Libby had fussed at him for messing up her clean floors with his blood, but then she held an ice pack to his face, cleaned him, gave him pain reliever, and made him take the rest of the day off while she pampered him, brought him food, and generally fussed over his wellbeing. He had pretended to chafe under her care, but secretly he enjoyed it. She was the only softness, the only tenderness in his life since his mother died, and he needed her, he realized with a jolt.

Before he could think it through, he flipped her hand over and kissed her palm. She blushed and dropped her gaze. Funny, he didn't ever remember seeing Libby blush before this summer.

"Have you ever kissed anyone?" he blurted.

She yanked her hand out of his grasp and turned her back to him, reaching for a dish to clear. "What a question."

"A question that's still awaiting an answer," he said.

"Not that it's any of your business, but yes, I've kissed people. What about you? Besides my sister, I mean." She turned to him over her shoulder with a raised eyebrow, as if to remind him of the impropriety of the conversation. Not that he needed a reminder.

He reached for the dishtowel and started to dry. Unbidden, the memory of Will helping Libby with the dishes popped into his head. Previously, he had felt disdain for Will for doing what he considered women's work. But now he wondered if he had simply been jealous of the time Will spent with Libby. After all, he was now helping her with the dishes, and he didn't feel at all odd about doing so. Rather, he felt thankful for the extra time with her.

"Anne was my first kiss and my only kiss for a long time. There have been others since." He didn't elaborate, and she didn't ask. "Your turn."

"I dated Marcus for a year."

His jaw dropped and he stared at her, waiting for more. Marcus Henshaw was the son of the richest rancher around, two years older than Dobbie, so four years older than Libby.

"When was this?" he asked when it became clear she wouldn't elaborate on her own.

"For the past year, until very recently."

"How recently?"

"Three weeks before you came home." She said it calmly, as if it meant nothing, but to Dobbie it was earth shatteringly significant.

The Henshaws were local celebrities because of their wealth, and Marcus was something of a catch.

"Why did you break up?" Was his tone normal? Or did it sound like he was trying to say the words through shards of broken glass, as it felt.

"We wanted different things," she said simply.

Dobbie heaved a sigh. "Libby, seriously, have you joined the CIA? Why are you being so closed mouth with me? We've never had secrets before."

"That's because you never tried to discover the inner workings of my heart before. A lady doesn't wear her emotions on her sleeve for all the world to see."

He paused to think about that. Libby had a strict code of conduct for herself about how a lady should think, and act, and feel, but where did it come from? Her mother died when she was ten. Surely she couldn't have learned all if it from her during those brief ten years. Anne didn't teach it to her. Anne was a cowgirl through and through with seemingly no emotion until her easterner showed up. He put the thought away to ponder later, adding it to the list of new questions he had about his life-long friend. He had the feeling it held the key to figuring Libby out.

"A friend confides in another friend," he said. "And I've been away a long time. I need to know what's going on with you."

"He wanted to marry me," she said in the same casual tone, but her words had the opposite effect on him.

"He what?" Dobbie thundered and tossed down the towel. Libby turned to look at him, her stoic silence a condemnation. Sighing, he reached for the towel again and forced himself to lower his voice. "It's possible I'm going to need more of an explanation than that."

"There's not much more to explain, Dobbie. He's twenty-two, and he wants to settle down. For whatever reason, he thought he wanted me. He said we could wait to get engaged until I turn eighteen, and then we could have a yearlong engagement."

"But you didn't want that," he said. Obviously she had been the one to break up.

She shook her head and focused on the dishes.

He clenched his teeth in frustration. Why was she making him drag everything out of her this way? Didn't she know she was making him crazy? Didn't she know his heart had stopped when she mentioned marriage to another man? He took her hands out of the water and turned her to face him. He would make her tell him what he wanted to know, and then he realized her eyes were brimming with tears. So instead of forcing her to talk he pulled her into a tight hug.

"Ah, Libby," he said, and her tears spilled over as her hands clutched his shirt.

With everyone else emotions made him uncomfortable, but with Libby it was the most natural thing in the world to comfort her. Her tears didn't scare him away, in fact they made a suspicious ache in his own chest, and he had a raging desire to fix whatever was making her cry. Even if it meant tracking down Marcus Henshaw and punching him in his smug face. In fact he rather wished it did. Marcus had had it coming for years, ever since he first laid eyes on Libby, as if she could ever be his, as if she could ever be anyone's but…

"Did he hurt you?" he asked. He mentally sized up Marcus Henshaw. They were equally matched, but with the way Dobbie was feeling now, he could easily rout him.

"He didn't hurt me," she assured him. "I hurt him. Everything has been in a muddle since you and Anne went away. I was so lonely, and it was nice to have someone to talk to and go out with, and then it snowballed and he was talking marriage, and I didn't know what to do, so I broke it off. I so badly wanted someone to talk to, to confide in and help me understand what was going on, but Anne wasn't here, and you… Do you think I did the right thing?" She looked up at him pleadingly with tear-wet lashes, and his heart turned over.

He framed her face with his hands. "Lib, did you love him?"

She was silent for so long as she stared at him his chest began to ache with an unknown dread. What if Libby loved Marcus? What if he proposed again and this time she said yes?

"I don't think so," she said slowly, too slowly for his liking, "but I've never been in love before. What does it feel like?"

He tried to conjure his feelings for Anne. They'd had a lot in common—their desire to build up the ranch, their die-hard work ethic, and their discomfort with anything emotional. When they talked, it was always about the ranch. When they kissed, it was always perfunctory and stilted, as if born out of duty instead of desire. What would it be like to kiss Libby? He stared down into her expectant face and had to use every ounce of self-control not to find out.

"I can't tell you," he choked at last.

Her look turned to sympathetic understanding. "She hurt you." She brushed her fingers on his cheek, soft as a whisper. "I'm sorry."

He swallowed hard. He wanted to tell her his strange reaction had more to do with her than her sister at this moment, but he couldn't, so he licked his suddenly dry lips and let her go. "Camping. We need to talk about camping."

"Camping," she agreed. She drained the water from the sink and led the way into the living room.

CHAPTER 5

*L*ibby sat on the couch and sighed wearily when Dobbie sat beside her. She was tired, but there were a million miles to go before bed. "How much thought have you put into this camping adventure, Mr. Dobbins?"

"I've spent hours mapping routes, testing campsites, and making lists of all the camping provisions we'll need," he bridled, somewhat defensive in response to her patronizing tone.

"Right. And the food," she said.

"That's your department." In truth the food situation concerned him, and when he couldn't figure out a solution, he dumped it on her. There was nothing, absolutely nothing she couldn't do.

"That's what I was afraid of. First of all, we're going to need plates, cups, and utensils for every camper."

"Not a problem," he assured her, glad to have some good news for once. "They're already on order."

"Good." She smiled approvingly, but it fled quickly. "Now comes the hard part. Somehow we have to pack ten days of meals for twelve people who will be eating three times a day. That's two hundred and fifty two meals we somehow not only have to pack, but keep fresh. Not to mention the problem of non-potable water."

He blinked at her a few times. Two hundred and fifty two meals. Somehow he had overlooked the math on that. And water? It hadn't even crossed his agenda. How were they ever going to carry that much food, let alone keep it fresh? "I have complete faith in you," he said, and he did. He touched his palm for the fourth time, and she noticed.

"Why do you keep doing that?" she asked.

"I have a splinter," he said.

"Why didn't you tell me sooner?"

"I thought I could get it out."

"Dobbie," she said irritably, and he smiled, glad to be back on familiar ground. "Stop picking at it and sit there quietly until I return with the first aid kit."

"Yes, ma'am," he said meekly. She left before he could see her smile and returned a few minutes later with a needle, alcohol, and antibacterial cream.

"I'm not using medicine for a splinter," he protested.

"You will, and you'll like it," she returned. She perched on the edge of the couch beside him, took his hand in both hers, and sterilized it with rubbing alcohol. She tilted his hand toward the light, trying to see the splinter. The sliver was in deep, and by the time she found the right light, she was teetering on the edge of his lap with her back to him. In the next room Kitty started to play a soft and pretty piece on the piano.

"There," Libby said, and held up the splinter, triumphant. "Why weren't you wearing your gloves, you crazy boy?"

"I was. It went through." He studied her profile as she worked over him, re-memorizing the graceful slope of her forehead and the pert tilt of her nose. The way her lips pressed together in total concentration, the way her ridiculous lashes fanned her cheeks when she blinked.

"Poor Dobbie," she murmured with uncharacteristic sympathy. She studied his hand as she rubbed the antibacterial cream into the small wound. His palm was large and rough with multiple calluses from many years of tugging ropes. Distractedly she finished applying the cream and then continued running her fingers over his hand as she inspected it. For some reason she thought of Will's hands. Will was her sister's boyfriend, and Libby had come to love him like a brother, but his hands weren't like Dobbie's. They were smooth and unblemished, the hands of a thinking man. She preferred Dobbie's hands, and the realization surprised her. For so long now she had thought her ideal man was someone like Will, someone who didn't know a bull from a steer. Maybe she could find someone like that who also had working man's hands. She smiled at her own fantasy because she knew it was one or the other, and she knew which one she belonged with.

"What's that smile for?" Dobbie asked in a mellow tone. His head was resting on the back of the couch, and he was thoroughly enjoying his unbidden hand massage.

"That's for me to know and you to find out. Allow a girl secrets, why don't you."

"Your maturity level astounds me, Miss Chapman."

"I'm a kid for a few more weeks, let me enjoy it."

"Fair enough," he agreed. "Let's do something special for your birthday."

"I was going to make a cake."

"You can't make a cake for your own birthday, Lib."

"I always do," she said matter-of-factly.

What else did she do uncomplainingly because it was her duty and there was no one else to do it? He had always thought Anne was the one who kept things going, but now he wasn't sure. After all, Anne declared ranch life wasn't for her and walked away. Libby was the one who kept the house running like clockwork and took care of them all. Any ranch hand could replace Anne, but who could replace Libby? The thought was disturbing on several levels, some he didn't understand and refused to peer closely into. He captured her hand and twined their fingers together, drawing her back against his chest so she was cradled against him.

"I want to take you out on your birthday, you and me. Something special."

"You do?" she asked, and the shy blush was back again.

"Yes, Lib."

"Why?"

"Because it's long overdue. We're friends, and you do so much around here with no thanks, and I want to do something nice for you." *And I'm dying to have a legitimate excuse to whisk you away and have you all to myself for a whole evening.*

"What will we do?" she asked. She settled back against his chest and absently toyed with his fingers. His hands were so much bigger than hers; they swallowed her fingers whole.

"Something special. It will be a surprise. Wear a dress for once."

"I'll see if I can pull one out of storage."

They sat holding hands in companionable silence until Libby realized he was asleep. She turned to study him. Tentatively, her hand reached out and skimmed softly over his forehead. He was very handsome, even more so when he was sleeping peacefully and not teasing her mercilessly as he was apt to. Like usual when she looked at him, her gaze focused on his lips. Not for the first time, she wondered what it would be like to kiss him, to have his beautiful lips on her mouth. Marcus had been good at kissing, technically capable and well-practiced. But it had never felt...right, never knocked her for a loop or made her brain turn to mush. Something told her if she ever kissed Dobbie, she would lose track of time and place.

She scowled and forced her thoughts away from his lips. It wasn't right to think of him this way. Dobbie was Anne's. No, Will was Anne's, she had chosen. But wasn't Dobbie still off limits to her because he had been her sister's first? And, if not for that reason, wasn't he off limits to her anyway? She wasn't cut out for ranch life. She wanted something more, but Dobbie didn't. He was where he belonged, but she wasn't. She was going away, and she didn't need anything else to tie her down to a life that already felt like shackles.

Dobbie twitched and his elbow knocked against his white cowboy hat sitting perched on the edge of the couch. Libby dodged across him to lunge for it and caught it before it could hit the ground. Her fast action startled him awake. He caught her around the waist and pulled her to his chest on instinct.

"Your hat was about to fall," she said. If it had been any other hat, she would have let it go, but it was the white Stetson her father bought him for his eighteenth birthday. Besides the fact it cost over a thousand dollars, it was a symbol of pride and family belonging, and Dobbie treasured it as his most valued possession.

"Thank you," he said. His gaze dropped to her lips but she didn't notice because her eyes fell to his lips, too.

"We'll need a mule," she murmured. Unbidden, her fingers reached out and touched his lips.

"What?" he asked and ran his thumb along her jaw.

"A mule," she tried again. "To carry the food for the trip. It will be too heavy for a horse."

"We don't have a mule, Libby." He closed the gap between them and placed a light kiss on the corner of her lips, almost but not quite touching her mouth.

She drew in a sharp breath. "I know that, Dobbie, but Marcus does."

He froze. "What did you say?"

She eased back from him slightly. "Marcus's family keeps mules. I'm sure they would let us borrow one."

He swallowed past the tightness in his throat. Now that he knew about her and Marcus Henshaw, he wasn't anxious to accept anything from him. On the other hand, she was right. They did need a mule, and he couldn't think of anyone else who had one. He let out a sigh and plopped his Stetson on his head.

"Why do you have to be so rational, Elizabeth?" He kissed her cheek and let himself out before he could do something crazy. Or something crazier than he'd already done.

CHAPTER 6

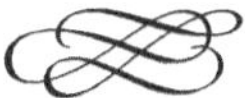

The next day Libby took inventory of her pantry and wrote down staple items she would need to purchase for the camping trip. She also made a list of questions to ask Dobbie as she thought of them. She would need to know about what they would encounter along the way, such as blackberry patches and wild greens to supplement their food supply. He would likely follow the mountain stream at the edge of the ranch, so she assigned Kitty to research the best way to make stream water potable. If they could do that, they wouldn't have to carry endless gallons of water, and it would be one less thing to worry about.

Kitty was a wizard at research, so Libby also had her look up ways to preserve fresh food on the trail. They would need to keep it away from bears, but she had every confidence Dobbie would know how to do that. Her focus was interrupted by a commotion outside, and she went to investigate. There stood Dobbie with a hacksaw in one hand and her goat in the other. She screamed, and he glanced at her in sharp surprise.

"What are you doing?" she raged. She stormed to the goat pen and slammed the door behind her.

"Cutting off its horns," he explained, as if they were discussing the weather.

"Why?" She lunged for the saw, but he held it away from her.

"Farm animals don't keep their horns, which you would know if you bothered to learn anything about ranch life. Plus it butted me in the leg and it hurt."

"These are cashmere goats, you bull-headed cowpoke," she ground through gritted teeth, hands on hips.

"So what?"

"So they have hot, thick coats. Their horns dissipate their body heat so they don't overheat and die, which *you* would know if you bothered to learn about *all* the animals on your ranch, and not only the cows."

"I know about the horses and the chickens, too," he said, flashing her a grin that stood out all the more in his grime-crusted face.

She didn't crack a smile. Instead she held out her hand. "Give me that saw, and don't ever touch my goats again."

He took a step toward her. "Ask me nicely."

"No." Her fierce tone lost something when she took a step back.

He caught her around the waist and drew her close, picking her up so her chest was pressed to his, her toes skimming the ground. "Ask me nicely, and I'll ignore your goats."

She swallowed hard. Why did he have to make everything so difficult? Why did he constantly have to push her buttons? "Please leave my goats alone."

"Say my name."

She wrinkled her nose at him and shoved down her irritation, knowing he wouldn't relent until she did it. "Dobbie."

"My real name, Elizabeth."

Libby hesitated. She didn't want to say it. Somehow in his arms, in the middle of her goat pen, it felt too intimate.

"Come on, Elizabeth," he coaxed gently, his words like a caress. "I can say your name, Elizabeth."

"Shane," she said, and her voice shook, along with her hands, which were now resting on his biceps.

He moved her even closer so their lips were almost touching. "When you said my name the other day, my real name, I wanted to..." He broke off because the mother goat was now butting him gently in his side.

"She thinks you're hurting me," Libby said and put out her hand to stop the goat.

"Am I?" he asked.

"No," she whispered. "You're not hurting me." She tilted her head to grant him better access to her lips.

He closed his eyes and tipped forward, but before he could reach her he froze and wrenched away, setting her away from him in the process. The tip of the goat's horn had caught his rib and poked, hard. Mustering a deep, cleansing breath, he handed the saw to Libby. "Good thing for you I'm a man of my word. Keep a closer eye on these, I found one of the kids in the yard because the gate was undone." He pivoted around her and let himself out of the pen.

After supper that night, Dobbie helped Libby with the dishes, as had become their habit. Unlike all the other nights, they didn't retire to the den to watch television when they were finished. Instead, he took her hand and led her outside.

"It's a nice night for a walk," he explained. They walked side by side, and she found herself agreeing with him. Her heirloom roses on the side of the house laced the night air with a sweet smell. The temperature felt right, and nearby crickets chirped at a furious tempo.

"It's seventy two degrees," Dobbie said.

"How do you know that?" she asked.

"The crickets. You count their chirps for fifteen seconds and then add thirty seven. It's not an exact science, but it's pretty close."

"Did Kitty tell you that?" Kitty was their resident expert in useless but interesting trivia.

"Nah. I learned it from an old cowboy. Cowboys know lots of

things." The way he said it, while darting a furtive glance at her, made her spine start to tingle.

Remembering their aborted kiss attempt in the goat pen this morning, she stopped abruptly and faced the house. "Maybe we should go back."

He clasped her other hand, linking them together. "Is that what you want, Libby?"

She hesitated as she stared up at him. It was a loaded question, and they both knew it. Did she want to go back to the way things had been, or did she want to keep going forward exploring this strange new atmosphere between them?

"I don't know," she said slowly.

"Let's keep going for a little while," he suggested.

She remained frozen another minute before turning to follow him again. He let go her hand and rested his arm companionably on her shoulders.

"The dog dug holes," he explained. "I don't want you to trip and twist an ankle."

She nodded and slipped her arm around his waist. "We should double up on the protection; I'm worried about the safety of my ankles."

He smiled and squeezed her shoulders. They walked in comfortable silence for a little while until they were out of view of the house and barns.

The horses were nickering in their stalls. Cows were lowing and, far away, she could hear her goats bleating. The sounds were comforting and familiar, and she paused to lean against a fence post and enjoy them.

"Did you miss the noises when you were away?" she asked. She closed her eyes and let the night sounds wash over her. The only sound more comforting was rain on their metal roof, her dad's voice, and Dobbie. Dobbie's laughter, Dobbie's teasing. The two years without his voice had been torture.

He studied her with her face tipped up to the moonlight, a happy smile spread on it, and thought how much he had missed her. "I guess

I never thought about it," he said. He itched to touch her and had to make himself focus on her words.

"That surprises me. The ranch is so much a part of you. I would have thought you would miss the sounds. I would miss them." She opened her eyes and looked past him, and he wondered if she was thinking about her unknown future.

"The sound I miss the most is one I'll never hear again," he said.

"What?" she asked softly, and, ever cognizant of when he might need comfort, took a step forward.

"My mom cooking breakfast in the morning," he said. He swallowed down emotion and fought for control. He would never tell her; but, sometimes in the early morning, he hung around the house and waited for the sound of her cooking breakfast because it was familiar and brought him comfort.

Libby rested her arm on the fence behind her. She looked at the pasture with a smile of fond remembrance. "When I was little, I always wanted to climb fences, but I was too afraid, and I didn't want to get my dress dirty. You and Anne made it look so easy, and so fun." She turned to look at him again, and he didn't give her time to react before he lifted her to sit on the fence rail in front of him.

She looked pretty with the moonlight glinting off her hair and face, and her long dress tucked under her as she perched on the edge of the rail. "You look like a postcard of a country girl," he said. He stood in front of her and rested his hands lightly on her hips to keep her from falling.

"Thanks, Dobbie." She shifted her position to try and straighten her dress. Despite his hands on her hips she started to topple forward and reached out her arms to catch herself on his shoulders. He righted her but she remained frozen with her hands on him. They paused and looked at each other for a long moment, feeling as if both their lives hung on what happened next.

Slowly she leaned down and pressed a kiss to each of his eyelids and then she stopped, hovering in front of his face, her breath mingling with his.

"Libby," he breathed. He leaned in to kiss her, freezing again when someone called to him.

"Boss." It was one of their ranch hands, a happy-go-lucky man named Caleb who was several years older than Dobbie, but still deferred to him as his leader.

"What is it, Caleb?" Dobbie asked, controlling his frustration with difficulty. He turned to look at the older man.

"That cow is calving, and we need you. I think we're going to have to pull it," Caleb said.

Dobbie sighed, and his shoulders sagged before he turned back to Libby.

She pressed her palm to his cheek. "I'll make you some coffee," she offered. The calving process could take a long time, and it would also take a lot of energy.

He smiled, his heart flopping. "Thanks, Lib."

Unbidden, Caleb reached up his arms to help Libby down. Dobbie scowled at him. "If you want to keep those hands, you'll put them back at your sides," he said.

Caleb gaped at Dobbie, shocked. Dobbie was rarely harsh or grumpy with the men. "Yes, Boss," he said, and dropped his arms list-lessly to his sides.

Dobbie held up his arms for Libby and lifted her down. They walked back to the house side by side with Caleb talking the whole way. Once at the door they parted reluctantly, their joined hands stretched out between them. Neither wanted the moment to end, for fear it might never come back around again.

"Calf," he said, nodding toward the barn.

"Coffee," she said, nodding toward the house.

"Later," he said.

"We'll see," she replied. She squeezed his hand, let him go, and went to make the coffee.

*L*ater that week, Kitty sat beside Libby in their old farm truck. It was an hour-long drive into town, and Kitty had volunteered to help Libby on the condition she also got to visit the library and get a new supply of books. As usual the younger girl had her nose in a book, and so it came as a surprise to Libby when she spoke.

"Dobbie's different," Kitty said. She didn't speak often, and when she did, it was usually well thought out and important. Like all the sisters, her eyes were brown, but they were flecked with green and gold. Of the four of them, her hair was the darkest, more of a chestnut color than light brown.

"What do you mean?" Libby asked, trying to keep her tone neutral. She didn't think her family knew anything that was going on between her and Dobbie, but her little sisters were sometimes more perceptive than she gave them credit for.

"Since he came home, he's different than before he went away. He laughs more, and he's softer now." She paused. "Come to think of it, I never remember hearing him laugh with Anne; I only ever remember hearing him laugh with you."

"He liked to tease me. He still does."

"Yes, but it's different now. I think he's falling in love with you."

Libby was saved from an emotional reaction by Kitty's cool and reserved tone. She always spoke as if she were a scientist stating a fact. "What makes you say that?"

"The way he watches you with his eyes all soft. It's the same way Will watches Anne."

Libby let out a breath. "I don't want him to fall in love with me."

"Have you told him you're leaving?"

"No."

"You should," Kitty said. "The longer you wait, the worse it's going to be."

Libby would have talked to her more, but Kitty opened her book and started to read again. That was the way it was with her little sister. She was an introvert and a thinker. She only had so much to give, and when it was gone, it was gone.

Libby, on the other hand, was more unsettled than ever, and her mind was going in twenty different directions. There were things she had to do to prepare for their tourists, but she had those written on a list. Besides, there was Dobbie. There were things she needed to tell him, but she didn't know how. And no matter what she did, she couldn't get him off her mind or out of her heart.

When they reached town, Kitty helped her unload her boxes of jam at the general store that had become a tourist haven. Many other ranches in town had also started accepting tourists, and the small town had blossomed under their influence.

"Hey, Libby," Mr. Smith greeted her. "I'm glad to see you. We're down to the last few jars of your jam. It's our most popular seller."

"Thank you, Mr. Smith. I'm glad to hear it." She arranged several jars on the shelf and helped him carry her boxes to the back storeroom. Kitty took off for the library as soon as her duties were over. Mr. Smith went to the cash register and paid Libby for the jam he had already sold on consignment for her. Her family knew she sold her jam, but if they knew how much she made, or how much she had in the bank, they would have been surprised. Her jams, along with her new cashmere wool business, were making her a tidy profit.

"I know I've said it before, but if you could do huckleberries, you would double your income," Mr. Smith said.

"I know, but Maggie is my berry picker, and our huckleberry patch is full of grizzlies, so you can see the problem. When we were little, Dad used to take us picking and stand guard with his gun because Mom loved huckleberries so much, but now," she paused and shook her head. She knew her tone was wistful, and she was embarrassed when Mr. Smith looked at her with something akin to pity.

"Your mother was a lovely lady," he said. "All sass and sunshine. Each of you girls got a little of her, I think."

"Thank you," Libby said, and her eyes shimmered with unshed tears.

"I heard Dobbie's back," Mr. Smith said as a way to lighten the mood. Unfortunately this threw her into even more emotional turmoil.

"Yes, well, he's our family, you know," she said awkwardly. Mr. Smith gave her an all-too-knowing smile.

"Maybe he could help you with the huckleberries," he said, and his eyes twinkled at her.

She could picture Dobbie standing guard with his shotgun, the way her father had done. He wouldn't let anything happen to her, or her sisters, but he would never do it. He would chalk it up as one more of her harebrained schemes, like the goats.

"I'll think about it," she said without much conviction. Her next stop was the large grocery store, and she commandeered two stock boys to help her with her purchases. By the time she picked up Kitty at the library, the back of the truck was overflowing with food and other items for the camping trip, and she was exhausted.

"There must be an easier way," she said to Kitty and dabbed at her upper lip with her handkerchief. No one sold handkerchiefs in the area so she ordered them off the Internet and embroidered them with her initials.

"Dad, Dobbie, and Will don't think so," Kitty said.

"Will? What's he got to do with it?"

"He's been looking over the books for Dad. He's good with finances, and he thinks the tourists might bring in enough money to get us out of the hole."

"How does Dobbie feel about Will helping?"

"Why don't you ask him?" She flashed her sister one of her rare saucy grins, and it was a reminder she had a sense of humor, quiet and studious though she was.

Libby returned her smile. "How much are we charging the tourists?"

"A thousand dollars each," Kitty said.

Libby's mouth fell open. "They're paying a thousand dollars to sleep outside and eat food cooked over a fire?"

"It's Montana," Kitty said. "Everyone's hoping to see a grizzly, or a wolf, or a beautiful mountain scene." Libby shook her head. It amazed her people would pay so much to come here when she was saving her money to get away. Still, the wheels in her head were turning. If they were willing to pay for camping, what else would they be willing to buy? One thing was for certain: she had a lot of work to do.

CHAPTER 7

The tourists were coming soon, and everyone felt it. Still, they all took a break to celebrate the fourth of July. It was Libby's bad luck their annual celebration was held at the Henshaw's sprawling ranch. Dobbie knew it was an annual event, but it didn't make his jealousy any less. Every year, the closest neighbors gathered at the Henshaw's for a picnic and fireworks. Close was a relative term when the nearest neighbor lived an hour away, but in this little corner of the country their gathering was composed of three families: The Henshaws, the Chapmans, and the Blakes. The Blakes had a daughter named Cecily who was Kitty's age, and the two girls were close. Their gathering used to include the Dobbins but since his parents died, Dobbie was their only remaining representative.

Libby added cooking for the party to her already too long list of things to do, but she traditionally brought certain dishes to the party, and she didn't want to disappoint anyone by not providing them today, so she spent days making pies, cupcakes, potato salad, baked beans, and homemade yeast rolls. Mrs. Henshaw provided the beef and iced tea, and Mr. Blake's cook sent a fruit salad and green beans. The Blakes were divorced and Mr. Blake had never remarried. The food was made in mass quantities because along with each family came all their ranch hands. So when Libby made cupcakes, she made eight-dozen cupcakes, and when she made potato salad, she made enough for one hundred people. She was exhausted by the time the Fourth rolled around, but being with their neighbors was such a rare event that her excitement outweighed her exhaustion.

Because of all the food and all the people, they had to take two cars and several horses. The hands rode their horses, and the family split into two cars. Dobbie and Libby ended up in a truck alone together, but Libby never learned if it was by chance or design.

"Libby, you're working too hard," Dobbie said. "You should delegate more to Maggie and Kitty. They're old enough now to start pulling their weight."

"They do pull their weight," Libby said defensively.

"Not as much as you do," he said.

When their mother died she and Anne had an unspoken agreement that Kitty and Maggie would be spared from as much work as possible. They both knew their mother would want their little sisters to remain carefree girls as long as they could. Libby assumed all of the household tasks while Anne did all of the outdoor work.

"Maggie helps me pick berries, and Kitty does research whenever I need it," Libby said. She was still feeling defensive. She had become a surrogate mother to her sisters, more so than Anne who had become a surrogate father when he closed up into his own grief-filled world.

"They're good girls, and I love them too, but it's not going to hurt them to help out more," Dobbie said. He was a part of the family and had no qualms about expressing his opinion or helping to discipline when it was required.

"That's right, they're girls, and I want them to stay that way as long as they can," Libby said. "I don't want them to have too much responsibility."

"Like you did," he said.

"I'm not complaining," she said.

"You never do," he said. He smiled at her and took her hand.

She looked out the window and smiled, too. Dobbie never complained, either. It was one of the things she liked best about him.

He had been shuttled to their home after the loss of his own home and family, and he took up the reins of responsibility on their ranch as if he had been born to it. She remembered the early days after his parents' deaths. He had thrown himself into work with a vengeance. Libby had expressed concern for him, but Anne said it was his way of dealing with the pain. Even so, Libby had given him extra portions at supper every night and made apple pie more often than usual for a long time after he came to live with them.

They arrived at the Henshaw's. Dobbie helped her carry all the food to the tables, and then he disappeared. Libby stuck close to Mrs. Henshaw and helped her arrange food and utensils on the long tables.

"Everything looks wonderful as usual, dear," Mrs. Henshaw said. She gave Libby what could only be described as a wistful look before turning away. Libby knew there was pressure on her and Marcus to make a match, even if it remained unspoken. Uniting their two ranches would create what amounted to an empire in Montana. Surely that wasn't the only reason Marcus had sought her out, was it? She hoped not. He had seemed to truly like her, and she had liked him. In fact, this was the first time she saw him after their breakup. Perhaps she should feel a bit more disconcerted over that fact, but she'd been too busy, first with one thing and then another.

Finally the food was arranged and everyone began to filter through the line. Libby stayed by the side of the table to refill or rearrange whatever needed doing. As the guests snaked through the buffet, she pondered the fact that so few of them were women. Besides herself and Mrs. Henshaw there was only Maggie, Kitty, and Cecily, compared to almost a hundred men. Things were old fashioned here, she thought. In most parts of the United States wealth, status, and power didn't matter much in the order of things, but here they did. The ranch owners had first dibs at eligible females, and the poor, non-land owning ranch hands came second. That meant Marcus had first claim to her, and all the other hands had to take a back seat to him. His younger brother Mathew was Kitty and Cecily's age, but he was eyeing Maggie, who was oblivious to him and talking horses with Mr. Henshaw.

She was the oldest eligible girl here, despite the fact that she was seventeen. People married young in these parts, and seventeen wasn't too young to get engaged. Several of the ranch hands were looking at her with interest, but she paid them no mind. A new thought came to her. Dobbie was considered a ranch hand, too. He was a foreman, which brought more status and respectability, but he had no land of his own. She didn't like to think of him that way, poor and somehow less than Marcus in everyone's eyes. He had owned land once and lost it by circumstance, did that make a difference? It made no difference to her one way or the other, she decided. Dobbie was Dobbie, and he would be the same poor or rich, and her feelings about him wouldn't change. Now the only problem was figuring out her feelings, she thought wryly.

She looked up as Dobbie passed. He caught her smile and winked at her, and her smile grew. In comparison to all the other cowboys she thought him the most handsome, but maybe she was biased. He was hers, no, scratch that. He was theirs. He was their Dobbie, and that made him better and more precious than all the other cowboys. She thought what he would say if he heard her call him precious and had to stifle her laugh.

All the men filtered through, and then Libby and Mrs. Henshaw filled their plates. They sat together with the other girls and listened to their happy chatter. Kitty and Cecily were opposites, and it was a wonder they were so close. Cecily was a flighty airhead who could barely keep her head on straight. She was slightly spoiled because her father doted on her, but she was still sweet and pleasant, and Libby liked her. She sometimes wondered if Maggie felt left out when the three of them were together, but quickly dismissed the idea. Maggie wasn't sensitive, and she didn't carry a chip on her shoulder. She made friends wherever she went and talked to whoever was available. Her favorite topic was animals, and she could usually find common ground with anyone.

She finished her meal, stood, and started to clean up, but Mrs. Henshaw shooed her away. "I have this, dear, why don't you take a walk?"

"All right," Libby said uncertainly. She wasn't one for walking around aimlessly by herself; she was more content to be working in the kitchen.

"That's a great idea, Mom," Marcus said from behind her. "Care to walk with me, Libby?"

"Sure." She gave him a shy smile and followed him from the barn. Despite the fact they had dated for a while, she had never learned to lower her guard completely with him, always keeping a part of herself in reserve. He had never seen her in a temper, for instance, once commenting she was the sweetest girl he knew. Dobbie would likely laugh at that statement.

They walked in silence for a few minutes. Libby wasn't sure how to read him, and she wondered if he was angry with her. Their breakup had only been a few weeks ago, after all. She had tried to do it gently, but no man liked to have his pride wounded by a girl.

"You look very pretty today, Libby," Marcus said at last.

"Thank you," Libby said. He had always been liberal with compliments, and she appreciated it. "Are you having a good season?"

"The best. At first I had trouble getting Dad to come around on some of the new things I learned at school, but then I pointed out to him he paid a large sum of money to my college, and if he was going to ignore what I learned, it was a poor value for his investment." He grinned. "You have to know how to talk to him on his level: All business, all the time."

"Sounds like my dad and Anne."

"And you," he added. "Most people don't know what a little business barracuda is hiding under that pretty face."

She flushed and looked away. "I forgot you knew me so well."

"Not as well as I would like," he said. He took her hand and wound their fingers together. He looked at her to see if she would refuse, but she didn't. Marcus was familiar and safe.

"Tell me about college, Marcus," she said. He, Anne, and Will were the only people she knew who had been to college.

"College was a lot of fun. It was a constant party, but I enjoyed the learning aspect, too."

"Do you think I would like it?"

He eyed her critically. "I don't know, Libby. It can get wild sometimes, and you're a sweet little flower. I would hate to see that taken away. I can't imagine you at a party."

"Surely not everyone parties, do they?"

"No, there were some people who didn't party. I don't know what they did for fun, though."

She turned away to hide her frown. It wasn't hard to picture Marcus as a partier, but she still didn't like it. He had been at college through most of their dating relationship. What, exactly, had he done and with whom? Even though they'd supposedly been exclusive, she was more concerned for his sake than jealous. As a neighbor and friend, she'd hate to see him stumble into anything that might lead to trouble. She tried to picture Dobbie at a party and couldn't. He wasn't a drinker and never had been.

"Are you as busy as ever?" he asked. Her busy schedule had been a source of contention between them. He accused her of being unavailable to him when they were dating. On the rare occasions he came home from college, he expected her to be available to dote on him. In a perfect world, maybe she would have been. Other girls her age seemingly had nothing better to do. But Libby had been far too occupied keeping house and growing her business ventures to dote over a boy, handsome and charming, though he had been and still was.

"Busier," she said, and squeezed his hand. "With the tourists coming, I don't have any idea how I'm going to get everything prepared. That reminds me, can I borrow one of your mules?"

"Don't tell me; you're starting a new venture that will combine goats and mules and make a million dollars," he said. He was always teasing her over her moneymaking projects, but in a good way, as if her ingenuity delighted him.

"No, nothing that exciting. We need a pack mule to carry food for the trip."

"No problem," he said easily.

"Thanks, Marcus. You Henshaws are good neighbors."

"And you Chapmans are easy on the eyes."

"I'll tell Dad you think so. He's been feeling down about his looks lately. This will help."

"Libby, sometimes I forget under your sweet exterior you're kind of rotten."

They walked in silence for a while, and Libby realized they had walked a long way and were at a remote portion of the ranch now. Her heels were sinking in the soft grass, so she reached down and plucked them off, allowing them to dangle from the tips of her fingers.

Marcus glanced at her in surprise. "I've never seen you take your shoes off before."

"I'm not sure we've ever gone walking like this before."

"Probably not. Our relationship was sort of a whirlwind of mixed agendas. We didn't take a lot of time to smell the roses, so to speak. We didn't take any leisurely strolls or steal into the barn to kiss in the hay." He stopped and faced her. "It's not too late. We just put out fresh hay." He smiled down at her and brushed a wisp of hair off her face.

She returned his smile. "Aren't all our friends and family still in the barn?"

"We have lots of barns," he said, and wagged his eyebrows at her.

She laughed until he advanced on her and backed her up against a fencepost.

"Marcus," she said breathlessly. "I don't think this is a good idea."

"Don't think about it, then. One kiss, Libby, please. I miss you." He put his hands on her waist and kissed her before she could protest or grant permission. He was an expert kisser, and before she knew what she was doing she dropped her shoes and kissed him back.

The kiss started to intensify, she finally returned to her senses, and broke it off. What on earth was she doing? "You said one," she said.

"That was one. It was long-lasting." He bent to retrieve her shoes for her. "I suppose I should get you back before the fireworks. Unless you'd prefer to stay and make our own?" He paused and gave her a searching look.

"I'm going to pretend you didn't say that," she said.

He sighed again, and she smiled. The remainder of their walk was pleasant and casual, and he didn't try to kiss her again, although he did remain attached to her side with a persistent sort of stubbornness.

When they returned to the barn the tables had been swept aside and the dance floor set up. Marcus claimed her for every dance. It was difficult to ignore Mrs. Henshaw's delighted glances in their direction. Libby looked for Dobbie, intent on offering him at least one dance, but he was nowhere to be found.

Fireworks happened after the dance, and Marcus sat by her during those, too. Once he tried to lean in for a kiss, but she turned her back slightly so he caught her shoulder.

"Cruel," he whispered, and she smiled. He helped her and Dobbie carry her now empty food containers to the truck, and he put up a hand to help her inside, but not before he kissed it.

Dobbie was silent and sullen for the first few miles.

"I didn't see you at all today," she said.

"Hmph," he grunted and wouldn't look at her.

"What does that mean?" she asked.

"I'm surprised you saw anything but his lips," he said.

She gasped. "Dobbie, you spied on us?"

"Yes, I did, and I got an eyeful."

"I don't believe you." Furiously, she turned toward the window.

"What, no comment on the kissing?" he asked.

"Oh, I have plenty of comments. You had no right to follow us and spy on us. That's, that's so…I don't have words for what that is."

"I had every right," he argued.

"You're going to have to explain that," she said.

"I," he paused and fumbled about for an explanation. "I'm responsible for you. It's my duty to keep an eye on you and your sisters; it's what your dad expects."

"And since when does Marcus fall under the jurisdiction of a suspicious individual?"

"Since he led you out to the middle of nowhere and kissed you senseless," he yelled.

"I was not senseless," she said, with equal venom and equal volume.

"You could have fooled me," he said.

"And you've kissed so many girls now in your vast experience that you know what senselessness looks like?" she asked.

"Yes," he said.

"That doesn't mean you can judge my level of senselessness. You have no idea what I look like when I've lost my head."

He slammed on the brakes, shifted the car into park, and turned to face her. "It's high time I changed that." He reached for her and pulled her so she slid across the seat and into his embrace. "Kiss him like that again, Libby, and I swear I don't know what I'll do." His mouth descended toward hers, but before he could reach her, someone knocked on the window.

Dobbie let her go and rolled down the window.

"What's wrong?" It was her father. They had forgotten he was in the truck behind them.

"Nothing," Dobbie said. "We...I was going to show Libby something."

Her father poked his head farther in the window and looked around. "What?"

"Nothing. It can wait. We'll see you at home." Dobbie rolled up the window, almost on her father's head, put the truck in gear, and started to drive.

Neither of them uttered another word for the remainder of the trip. He slammed out of the truck as soon as they arrived. She thought he was angry, but then he came around to her side, opened her door, and lifted her down.

"Rain check," he whispered, and helped her carry her containers inside.

CHAPTER 8

There was no longer enough time in the day. Libby planned menus, made endless lists of what needed to be done, and then did it. Her garden was starting to bear fruit and she pickled and canned almost from sunup to sundown some days. She was so busy she barely saw or spoke to Dobbie, but it was a bit of a relief. They were both getting a much-needed break from the horrible tension that simmered between them.

One morning, a week before the tourists were set to arrive, Libby went out to feed her goats, and her heart sank. One of the kids was missing. She made a frantic search of all the barns and almost ran head first into Dobbie, who grabbed her upper arms to keep her from falling.

"What's wrong?" he asked, his concern for her was evident in his tone and expression.

"One of my kids is missing," she said. "I think they learned how to open the gate." Tears pooled in her eyes and threatened to spill over.

"I'm sorry, Libby," he said sincerely. "I know how much they meant to you."

The way he said it in the past tense and with such finality annoyed her and she shrugged away from him. "I'm going to look for her."

"You can't go by yourself. Those woods are massive, you'll get lost." There were thousands of acres, and she rarely set foot outside the house. "You have zero sense of direction and no survival skills."

She gave him the doe eyes, and his tone turned pleading. "Libby, no, I'm busy. I can't take the day off to search for one of your stupid goats when it's probably already been picked off by a wolf or a bear."

"Fine." She tipped her head in the haughty, determined way he recognized, shoved past him, and disappeared into the house. When she reemerged a little while later, she was wearing jeans and looked surprised to see him sitting on his horse and holding out the reins of Maggie's pony to her.

"Who knows you better than me?" he asked, falling silent to watch her swing up into the saddle. He whistled. "Nice form."

She grinned at him. "You live on a ranch your whole life, you pick up a thing or two."

He couldn't seem to take his eyes off her. "I didn't know you owned denim."

She looked down at pants. "I don't. They're Anne's."

Anne had never looked that classy in them, he thought. Somehow she had transformed even jeans to fit her own style. They were cuffed up to her calf, and she wore a short-sleeved button up shirt with a jaunty scarf tied at her neck.

"Hold on a minute," she said. She threw him her pony's reins, ran back inside, and came back a while later carrying food and water and wearing her own white Stetson. He didn't tell her he had already packed food. Hers was probably better anyway.

"Which way, Annie Oakley?" he asked.

She looked around. "She would probably head toward vegetation."

"My thoughts exactly." He headed in the direction of a thick copse of trees off in the distance. Beyond that was their mountain and grizzly bears. But she wouldn't allow herself to think of that. Thankfully Dobbie refrained from voicing the futility of the situation.

"Why are these goats so important to you?" he asked instead.

"Because they're mine," she said.

"Everything on the ranch is yours."

"No. I bought these with my own money, money I earned all by myself. They're my own business venture, and I won't fail. Plus, I need all their wool, even the two kids."

"For a little wisp of a thing, you're very driven."

"I prefer to call it passionate, Mr. Dobbins," she said and gave him a wink before urging her pony forward.

He grinned at the back of her head and caught up with her. Occasionally he paused to observe an almost imperceptible path through the woods. She was glad he was there because she would never have picked up on it, and she would be hopelessly lost.

"I haven't ridden out here since I was a little girl and used to ride with Dad," she said. "It's so beautiful."

"It is that," he agreed. He had been a lot of places, but nothing compared with Montana. He was glad it was his home.

"Tell me about the girls after Anne," she said.

"You don't want to hear about that," he said.

"If I didn't, I wouldn't have asked," she said.

He let out a protracted sigh. "I was hurting and angry, I guess, and surprised to learn girls found me attractive. You four are the only girls I've ever known." He paused thoughtfully. He realized he had compared all the girls he met to the four Chapman sisters, and everyone else came up lacking. "I found a new girl everywhere I went, to see if I could. There were all different types of them."

"But no one special," she guessed.

"No one special," he agreed.

"Because of Anne? Did you hope when you came back that she had changed her mind?"

He paused. Did he think that? Had he been hoping to find Anne waiting for him? "I don't think so, I felt driven to come home, like if I didn't get here I might explode." In reality the first person he thought of when he returned was her. He knew she would be in the kitchen, and he made a beeline for it as soon as he spoke to her father. Even as he spoke to Matt he had felt antsy and distracted, as if he couldn't rest until he saw Libby, and when he did, his whole world had imploded. He glanced at her in alarm. Could it be that all the restlessness he felt the last two years was because he was away from *her*, and not the ranch? He swallowed hard and focused forward again.

"Why were you so upset I went away?" he asked. They had bantered as adversaries and loved each other in their way, but they hadn't been close.

"I don't know. It took me by surprise. I thought I would be relieved, but then it happened so unexpectedly, and I felt empty all of a sudden. One day I was scrubbing the floor a week after you went away, and I burst into tears because there was no more mud to clean up." She paused. "You had always been with us, every day since I was twelve, and then when you weren't anymore, I realized how much a part of me you had become."

They rode in silence a while. "I missed you, too," he admitted eventually. "Every dress or cleaning product I saw reminded me of you."

"Great. Dresses and cleaning products, that's my legacy."

"It's a great legacy, Lib," he said sincerely. "Every time I see something pretty or feminine or good smelling, I think of you. All I have to make you think of me is dirty boots on your clean floor."

"And bloody noses," she added.

"And bloody noses," he agreed.

And sensuous, full lips, and rough masculine hands, and horses, and leather, and laughter, and teasing, and a wealth of other things that almost overwhelmed her with their connection to him.

"You're quiet all of a sudden," he said. "It makes me crazy trying to figure out what you're thinking. Once upon a time I thought I had you all figured out."

"Same goes for me," she said. "Once upon a time you were only a simple country boy."

"I'm still only a simple country boy," he said.

"Maybe in some ways, but in others you're so much more."

"Do tell," he urged, but she only smiled in her usual mysterious way.

He let out a long and frustrated sigh, and she laughed. Why had he never noticed how beautiful her laugh was before? She was captivating, and he was torn between his need to blurt out his growing attraction to her and the need to flee for self-preservation. Instead, he kept silent. They rode for a long time, until he sensed she needed a break. Anne could ride all day with no discomfort, like him, but Libby was unused to the saddle.

"You're going to be sore tomorrow," he said, and put up his hands to help her down.

"I'm sore now." She rested her hands on his chest and allowed him to take her weight as he set her on her feet. Being on a horse was a little like being on a boat, and it took a minute to get her land legs back.

"Okay?" he asked, his hands settled at her waist.

She slid her hands up to his shoulders. "Give me a minute."

"Take all the time you need," he said, and they smiled because they both knew she was fine. But they were alone in the woods with a goat on the loose. Now wasn't the time. He chucked her under the chin and let her go. She stretched for a bit and began setting out lunch.

When Dobbie came back from using the facilities in the woods, he laughed at the sight before him.

"What's so funny?" Libby asked.

"You brought a tablecloth."

"So?"

"You're cute, Libby, and you don't even know how cute you are."

She sat up primly and handed him a moist wipe to clean his hands. "A lady is a lady no matter where she goes," she said primly.

"Amen to that," he said, and squeezed her knee before she slapped his hand away.

"Don't patronize me," she said.

"I'm not, I promise. I like the way you are."

She wrinkled her nose. "*The way you are*. That makes me sound like I have a disease."

"You're unusual, but I wouldn't have you any other way."

"Newsflash, mister: you don't have me now," she said and handed him the plate she'd prepared for him.

"I don't think a lady is supposed to wound the ego of a gentleman," he said.

"You're right. Find me a gentleman, and I'll be careful with his fragile ego."

"Big words from a girl who is now dependent on me for her survival," he said.

"Says the man who is eating my delicious food," she said.

"It is delicious. No one cooks like you, Libby." He paused to take a bite. "Want to hear a secret?"

"Always."

"One of the reasons I was looking forward to marrying Anne was so I could move into the main house and be closer to your cooking."

She smiled, but it soon fled. "I'm sorry, Dobbie, truly." She reached out her hand to clasp his.

"You say it like it was your fault, Libby. You didn't have anything to do with it."

She stared at their joined hands. "But I wanted Will to win Anne."

He reached out and took her other hand. "Why?"

"Because they fit somehow, and because…because the thought of you and Anne together made me sad in a way I couldn't understand." She kept her eyes on their joined hands, too ashamed and embarrassed to look at him.

"Sad. What an interesting emotion to have in that situation."

She tugged her hands out of his and stood before the conversation could get any more uncomfortable. "Let's find my goat." She packed up their things and swung up into the saddle before he could help her, and then started off before he could get to his horse.

Despite her head start their progress was slow. Libby was in pain, and the brush was thick. Occasionally they found little clumps of goat hair but no blood, so Dobbie thought the goat was still alive and they kept going. As they rode closer to the mountain the weather started to shift and clouds began to gather overhead. It often happened that the mountain's weather was different than anywhere else. Dobbie grabbed her reins before the first clap of thunder sounded, and it was a good thing because her pony reared slightly, and it took Dobbie's powerful mastery to keep him under control.

He held her reins until she dismounted, and then he dismounted his own gelding. He tied them to a tree and fished out a large plastic tarp as the first raindrops fell.

They sat huddled together on soft pine needles with the tarp drawn tightly around them. The rain was too loud for conversation, but the silence was intimate and cozy, and neither of them minded that it rained for a long time. The rain and the wind made it cold and Libby shivered. Dobbie wrapped his arms around her shoulders, and she wrapped her arms around his waist. She pressed her head against his chest and closed her eyes, glad he couldn't see how much she was savoring the moment. Then she wondered if he was enjoying the reprieve as much as she because he scrubbed his chin on the top of her head a couple of times and tightened his arms, inhaling deeply.

When it was over, they waited for a few minutes to see if it would start again. At last the sun appeared, and Dobbie stood to shake out the tarp. He checked the sky and noted the position of the sun.

"We'll go a little farther and then make camp for the night."

"Camp," Libby exclaimed. "We can't camp out here. We have to go back."

"We can't make it home before nightfall, and you're not experienced enough to ride in the dark."

"But we can't stay out here." She looked around frantically, hating the note of desperation in her tone.

"Why not? I've done it hundreds of times."

"With a girl?"

"Sometimes with Anne when we had business to attend to. It's awkward but unavoidable."

"Do you have a tent?"

"A tent. Sweetheart, you're adorable."

"We don't have food, either," she pointed out.

He lifted his saddlebag to show her his provisions, and she wrinkled her nose. "Canned beef stew can hardly be considered food," she said.

"Beggars can't be choosers," he said. He was starting to get annoyed and she sensed it, so she closed her mouth and climbed on her horse. Fear kept her too distracted to watch for her goat, but she knew Dobbie was looking.

Dobbie noticed her unnatural silence but chalked it up to fatigue. Dusk started to settle and he found a good spot to camp. He had used it a few times before when he came this way. Now he settled his blanket roll on a bed of pine needles, took the saddle blanket off his horse, and spread it nearby. He used clumps of grass to rub down his horse and smiled approvingly at Libby when she did the same for her pony. She might not be a bona fide cowgirl, but she knew the rules of proper animal care. She helped him collect a few sticks of dead wood and leaves and, after a few failed attempts, he had a small fire going.

Libby disappeared into the woods, presumably to use the facilities, but when she returned she had the makings for a salad. Dobbie watched while she used his knife to cut up wild carrots, fiddlehead fern, and wild onion, and then crushed blackberries over it to make a dressing. He stared at their shared plate, too fascinated to eat it.

"How do you do that?" he asked, awed.

"What?" she asked distractedly as she opened the can of stew and scooped it onto his plate.

"How do you make everything look so perfect and beautiful and, well, special? You can take something as ordinary as weeds and make them look interesting and appetizing."

She wasn't aware she was doing anything unusual. "I don't know. I guess I make it look the way I want it to look and hope for the best."

"Incredible," he whispered and held up his fork between them. "I only have one."

"You go ahead. You have a bigger appetite."

He speared a forkful of salad and held it out to her. "We'll share, ladies first."

She opened her mouth but caught his hand before it could reach her. "Did any of those many girls you kissed have a disease I'm going to catch?"

"Gross, Libby, what do you take me for?"

"Tell me their last names," she challenged.

"Fine, I got a bit carried away there for a while, but all the girls were clean and lacking festering lip wounds. Satisfied?"

She opened her mouth again, and he shoved the food in.

"Did you ruin all your romantic moments with Marcus this way?" He loaded the fork again and took a bite of salad. It was delicious, as he knew it would be.

"No, I never ruined a romantic moment with Marcus," she said softly. At his dark expression she hastened to add, "We never had any this romantic," and then took the bite of food he offered.

After they ate, he banked the fire and she sat back, exhausted. During supper she had been able to pretend they weren't in the middle of the wilderness, but now darkness was fully descended, and the night sounds were overwhelming.

"We should go to sleep," Dobbie said, yawning. "We can start again at daybreak." He stretched out on his saddle blanket and laid his rifle beside him. The gun brought her some reassurance. Her father and all the ranch hands carried rifles powerful enough to take down an elk, bull moose, or even a grizzly, although, no one had ever had to do it. The grizzlies were shy and usually a warning shot was enough to scare them off.

But what if it wasn't? What if a grizzly stumbled upon them while they were sleeping? They cleaned all traces of food from the campsite, but bears had powerful noses. What if they missed some crumbs and a bear followed the scent? It could have the drop on them before Dobbie could get to his gun, despite his proficiency with the weapon.

Libby was exhausted, but she couldn't seem to turn off her mind or quash her anxiety. All the what-ifs in their situation rushed up to greet her and kept her staring unblinking at the half moon. Far away a wolf howled, and then another, and another. Were they talking about Dobbie and her? Were they tracking them, waiting for a moment of weakness?

Silent tears ran unchecked down her face, and she started to tremble. She thought Dobbie was asleep until he said her name.

"Libby, are you crying?"

"No," she sniffled.

He inched closer to her so he could see her face in the moonlight. "You are. What's wrong?" His tone was tenderer than she had ever heard it, and her crying increased.

"I'm scared."

"Come here, sweetheart," he said, and opened his arms to her. She buried her face in his chest, and he wrapped her tightly in his comforting embrace. As if by magic, her tears dried up. He was solid and warm, making it impossible for her to hold onto her fear.

"I'm sorry," she muttered.

"Why?"

"Because I'm not cut out for this sort of thing."

"Why should you be? It takes practice. It doesn't come naturally." He smoothed his hand along her hair.

She couldn't help saying what she was thinking. "Anne could do it. She did it all the time. She was never afraid."

He paused while he thought that over. "Yes, Anne could do it. She could ride in the saddle all day without wincing, and she could make camp and sleep under the stars all by herself. She could pull calves and brand them, even better than I could, but you know what?"

She shook her head.

"She didn't need me. There was nothing I could do for her she couldn't do for herself. I like the fact that you need me here to protect you and lead you home. I like the fact that you're soft and sweet and delicate. It makes me feel good to take care of you, and I will take care of you, you know that, right?"

"Yes, I know that, but what if a bear attacks while we're asleep?"

"Bears have to sleep, too, you know." Grizzlies were nocturnal, but there was no need to share that information with her, especially when she relaxed in his arms and he felt her fear ebb away.

"Sometimes I wish I was brave like Anne."

"What do you think Anne would do if you told her to cook supper and can the leftovers?" he asked, and she giggled.

"Good point, but cooking can be learned. Courage can't."

"Just because you're not outdoorsy doesn't mean you don't have courage. Who taught you how to cook, bake, can, sew, quilt, and knit?"

"No one. I taught myself."

"Right, you learned because there was no one else to do it, and so you did it. That's courageous."

"Camping Dobbie is sweet," she said.

"Maybe Libby's Dobbie is sweet," he suggested, nestling her impossibly closer.

"Libby's Dobbie," she repeated. "I like that."

"So do I, sweetheart, so do I." He kissed the top of her head, and a few minutes later they were both asleep.

CHAPTER 9

Libby woke at the crack of dawn. She had slept dreamlessly, and she felt refreshed, despite the fact that she was sore all over from her long stint in the saddle and a hard night on the ground. Dobbie was still asleep, and she was surprised. He often suffered from insomnia and was usually awake before the rooster crowed, figuratively speaking because their rooster crowed all the livelong day.

His arm was slung over her and curled around her head in a protective embrace, and she smiled. Dobbie oozed protectiveness. He liked to take care of people, and caring came naturally to him. It came naturally to her, too, and she liked to take care of him because no one else did. Before, when he and Anne were together, her sister never seemed to notice Dobbie's needs. It wasn't that she was self-absorbed. No, Anne was a loving, giving person once you got to know her. It was that she didn't seem to think Dobbie had any needs. She missed the hungry way he hovered on the periphery of their family, dying for a scrap of affection, too proud to ask. She never seemed to notice the loneliness that hovered around him when he rode fences by himself. At times Libby had actually chastised her for her callousness toward Dobbie, but Anne would always look at her in confusion.

"Dobbie's the happiest guy I know," Anne would say. "He's always smiling."

But Libby saw behind the smile to the sad and lonely orphan he was.

"I'll take care of you," she whispered, so low the words barely formed.

"You always do," Dobbie murmured, and pulled her slightly closer. His eyes opened, and she was amazed by the amount of affection she read in them. She wondered if it was the same way she was looking at him. She figured it probably was because neither of them looked away.

"You're a pleasant sight to wake up to," he said.

"Don't get attached. Dad will have your hide."

"Don't I know it, but I actually slept last night. No nightmares."

She pressed her palm to his cheek. "What are your nightmares about?"

"The fire," he said. His face contorted with pain, and she smoothed her hand over his forehead. He had lost both his parents in a house fire when he was fourteen.

"Can you tell me?" she asked.

"I don't know. I've never talked about it." He swallowed hard. "I don't remember much. I swallowed a lot of smoke, and spent a few days in the hospital."

She remembered. Her family visited him every day, all the neighbors had. Libby had taken him cookies.

"The one thing I remember is the one thing that haunts me." His hands turned into a painful grip. "I stumbled out of the house and called for my dog." He swallowed hard again. "My parents were dying, and I was calling for my dog." He buried his face in her shoulder and shuddered with the effort it took not to cry.

"Shane, you were confused and disoriented by the fire, the smoke, and the panic. You weren't thinking rationally. No one could in that situation. It's okay. If you could go back as the man you are at this moment, you would go to your parents and pull them out, and nothing would stand in your way, I know it. But you were a confused and injured boy. There was nothing you could have done, nothing. Dad said they died in their sleep and didn't suffer."

During her speech he started to relax, but he didn't pull his head away from her shoulder. Instead he moved slightly so his lips were on her neck, and she drew in a shaky breath.

"We shouldn't."

"I know. For a thousand reasons I know, but I don't care. I want to. I need to. I need to kiss you, Libby, don't you feel it?" He pulled back to look at her. "Don't you feel this force drawing us together? I'm tired of fighting it all the time."

"Then don't," she said before she could change her mind.

"Libby," he breathed. He closed his eyes and touched his lips to hers, and then they heard it—the insistent bleating of a goat. "You have got to be kidding me." His lips moved against hers.

"That's what you get for terrorizing my goats. They'll always get even." She kissed the tip of his nose and jumped up to follow the sound of her bleating kid.

It was less than thirty feet away and stuck in some heavy brush. It appeared weak but otherwise unharmed. Dobbie checked it over and declared it to be dehydrated. Libby gave it some water and after a few minutes it perked up. Dobbie used his knife to cut away the entangling brush while Libby tied a rope around its neck.

"Where did you learn to tie a rope like that?" Dobbie asked.

"You date a cowboy for a year, you learn things," she said.

He stood straight and scowled. "What else did you learn?"

"Maybe I'll show you sometime." She patted his cheek, breezed by him, and mounted her pony.

He gave a sharp tug on the goat's rope to lead him. "If not for you, she might have shown me this morning," he said. When the goat looked up at him, he could swear it was smiling.

"Come on, you worthless pest." He tied the goat to the back of Libby's saddle, mounted his horse, and set off. It was a hot day, and they were both hungry and thirsty so they didn't talk much. When they finally arrived home in the late afternoon, Libby placed her goat in the pen and wrapped extra wire around the fence to secure it.

Dobbie sat at the kitchen table, his head resting in his hand. Libby poured them each a glass of iced tea and made them sandwiches. They ate in silence, but when she stood to clear their plates, he grasped her waist and pulled her close.

"You and I have some unfinished business," he said, and her spine began to tingle.

"Yes, we do," she agreed. She cupped his face with her hands. "Thank you for helping me get my goat back." She pressed a kiss to his forehead and pretended to walk away, but of course he pulled her back.

"I'm going to need more thanks than that," he said.

"What did you have in mind?" she asked. The front door opened and slammed. By the time her father entered the kitchen she was at the sink with the faucet running.

"I need to talk to you," Matt Chapman said to Dobbie, turned, and stormed from the house without waiting to see if his order was followed.

"Here it comes." Dobbie stood and pushed his chair back, then noticed Libby heading out, too. "Where do you think you're going?"

"With you," she said, as if it were obvious.

"Oh, no you don't. He said he needs to talk to me."

"And I'm going with you."

"No, you're not."

"Try and stop me." Her head rose in the gesture he knew all too well. He quickly ran through all the ways he could try to stop her, and while some of them might be fun, none of them would work. Once Libby had her mind made up, there was no changing it. Instead of arguing, he clasped her hand and led her out of the house.

"Fine." He let her go before they reached the barn. Whatever was coming, they both knew it was better if they didn't appear to be together.

Libby's father scowled when he saw her. "I wanted to talk to Dobbie alone." She raised her chin, and he cast his eyes heavenward. His wife had that same look, and he knew it well. He ignored her and turned to Dobbie.

"I cannot believe my ranch foreman left off work for two days to go gallivanting around the countryside looking for a goat," he yelled furiously.

"Dad," Libby started, but Matt turned on her. "And you, sleeping out all night with a man. You are grounded, young lady."

She actually laughed at that. His fury increased, and it notched up her own temper. "Grounded from what? The garden? My pressure canner? You may have noticed I don't go anywhere or do anything. And why are you angry about camping? Anne and Dobbie did it all the time, and they were dating."

"That was different," her father said.

"How?"

He had to think about that for a minute. Why did the thought of Libby with Dobbie all night under the stars bother him when the thought of Anne with Dobbie hadn't given him pause? He looked curiously between the two youngsters before answering. "That was ranch business."

"This was ranch business," Libby said.

"It was a goat," her father said.

She clenched her fists at her sides. "Does no one listen to me? They are cashmere goats. *Cashmere.* Do you have any idea how valuable their wool is?"

"No," her father said. "Tell me."

She named a figure that made Dobbie and Matt's mouths drop.

"Although, I'm barely getting started and building up my herd. It's going to take a while before they turn a hard profit."

"And who is going to take care of them in the fall when you go to college?" her father demanded.

Libby's eyes flicked apologetically to Dobbie. He looked stricken, betrayed, and angry.

"Maggie," she said, still watching Dobbie who would no longer meet her gaze. "She's going to feed them and brush them and save the wool for me. I'll spin it and card it when I'm home on breaks." She looked back at her father who was once again glancing between her and Dobbie with deepening suspicion.

"And what happens if you don't come home?" Dobbie asked in a hard, clipped tone.

Her eyes settled back on him. "I don't know," she said, unsure if they were still talking about the goats.

Her father let out a breath and relaxed his stance, eager to turn his mind to a safer subject. "Fine. From now on the goats are considered part of the ranch, and I'll have one of the boys secure their pen better. As for you two," he paused and watched the tension between them with a combination of concern and elation. "Just be careful." He turned and left the barn before things became any more awkward, but he needn't have worried because Dobbie turned to go at the same time.

Libby hurried forward to lay her hand on his arm, but he shook her off and kept walking, so she jumped on his back before he could exit the barn.

"What do you know, jeans do have an advantage," she said, securing her legs around his waist like a koala.

He couldn't help but smile. Everyone thought she was so sweet, and she was. But she was something more; Elizabeth Chapman was all spirit and passion. He pressed her back against an empty stall and leaned on her so his head rested on her shoulder.

"You could have told me," he said. He slid his hands up to rest on her forearms, which were clasped about his neck.

"I could have. I should have, but I just got you back, and things have been strange between us."

"Yes, things gave been strange." He closed his eyes and drew in a deep breath. He caught the scent of strawberries and almost groaned. She couldn't leave; he couldn't bear it.

"Does it really matter?" She traced his ear with her index finger. Even when he was angry with her, she felt a compelling need to touch him. "We've been doomed from the beginning. We're too different, and we both know it. We have no future and too much past and present to risk something casual and fleeting."

She was right, but it didn't make it hurt any less. "Where does that leave us?" he asked.

"The same as ever. Friends. Family. Two sad people with amazing chemistry and nothing to do with it."

At least it was out in the open now, and it was mutual. "I've never wanted anything more than I want to be with you, Libby."

He felt her heartbeat quicken, and his echoed a response. "That goes double for me, Shane." She kissed his cheek and rested hers against his.

He opened his eyes. "I can't be with you and not together." He picked up her hand and kissed her palm. "I can't even turn around right now because I know I'll kiss you, and once won't be enough. I need some space."

"I understand. The camping trip is in a few days, I'm going to be swamped preparing for it, and then you'll be gone for a week. That should help."

He nodded, but he wasn't convinced anything could help at this point. "Goodbye, Libby."

"Goodbye." She unclasped her arms and legs and stood to watch him walk away.

CHAPTER 10

The few days before the tourists arrived were pandemonium. Even Kitty and Maggie got sucked into the mayhem of preparation. Libby was sure she had never worked harder in her life. She was functioning on less than four hours of sleep, and she knew it was the same for Dobbie.

The one break in her whirlwind of activity came in the form of Marcus Henshaw. She thought he would send one of his cowboys with the mule, but she was wrong.

At the sight of him stepping from his truck, her hand fluttered nervously to her hair. Marcus was the epitome of everything she once thought she wanted in a man. He was handsome, rich, cultured, well mannered, and educated. His father was wealthy enough to send him away to college and still maintain enough help on his ranch during his absence, so Marcus had obtained a four-year degree in animal husbandry, and was already employing new techniques on his family's ranch.

He ignored Libby until he had the door of the trailer opened. Then he turned to her with a smile. "He doesn't want to come out."

She descended the porch steps and went to stand next to him at the opening of the trailer. She could see the mule staring out, stubborn and scared. "Hi," she said to the mule. "I'm Libby. You're going to stay with us for a few days, and then you're going to go home, but we'll take good care of you. Won't you come out?" She held out her palm to him, and he edged his way out. "That's a good boy," she said and scratched behind his ears. He gently butted her shoulder a few times when she stopped, urging her to continue.

"Looks like you have a friend for life," Marcus said. "I see now why your father keeps you away from his beef cows. You would cry on market day."

"My tears would dry quickly when I saw all the money."

He gave her a warm smile. "Where do you want this guy?"

"How do you feel about goats?" she asked the mule, and led him to the goat pen. The goats bleated at him, but in a friendly way. He pricked his long ears at them.

"I think they'll be all right together," Libby said. She turned and gasped in surprise when Marcus pinned her against the trailer and rested his hands on her waist.

"I've missed you, Libby. I know I rushed you and pushed you, and I'm sorry, but we can go back. We can date casually, and I won't press for more."

She opened her mouth, but no sound came out, and he pressed his fingers to her lips.

"I know you have a lot on your mind with the tourists. I'll give you some time to think it over." He crooked his finger under her chin, tipped her face up, and kissed her lightly on the lips.

She kept her eyes closed until he started to drive away, and then she opened them. While the trailer had blocked the view from the house, it did nothing to hide them from the barn, and now Dobbie stood in the entryway watching her with an inscrutable expression. Their eyes caught and held for a minute before he turned and walked away.

The next morning everything was finally in order. Libby stayed up all night, going over and over her supplies and checklists until she was finally satisfied she hadn't missed anything. The mule was ready, and their cook, Hank, was set to arrive on his own horse any minute. Libby tried not to feel anxious, but she would be glad when the group was on its way and she could finally relax and get some sleep.

The van Dobbie had rented to pick up the tourists pulled up the long lane, and Libby, Kitty, and Maggie went out on the porch to greet them. Their father was busy in the pasture. With Dobbie taking the week off to lead the trip, Matt couldn't spare the time to greet their guests.

Dobbie had a charming side to his nature, and it was in full force today. Libby looked at the small crowd of tourists and felt secretly glad none of them were young and pretty. He came up the steps, took her hand, and led her down to the waiting group. His eyes were trying to tell her something, but she didn't know what.

"This lovely lady is my partner in crime," Dobbie said. "She'll be coming with us as our cook, but don't let her age fool you; she's the best cook in the state." He squeezed her hand to keep her from gasping at his statement and raised her hand to his lips while his eyes pleaded with her to go along with what he was saying.

"Is she your sweetheart?" one of the older men asked.

Dobbie looked at her, trying to find an answer. "She's my best friend," he said, and Libby dropped her gaze and blushed while the watching crowd said a collective, "Awww."

One of their ranch hands, Toby, led them to their horses, and Dobbie moved closer to whisper in her ear. "Hank broke his leg last night. You're going to have to come."

She knew her eyes were filled with panic. "I can't."

He put his hands on her shoulders. "You have to, Libby. There's no one else."

Her eyes swam with tears, and she looked away. Besides the fact she was exhausted from lack of sleep, she was terrified of sleeping outdoors, and she had no idea how to cook over an open fire. It was a learned skill she didn't possess. She knew for sure she was going to fail and let Dobbie down, and that was the worst part. Still, he was right; there was no one else. She wiped her eyes and squared her shoulders. "All right. I'll need a minute to gather some things."

"I'll keep them busy for an hour while you pack," he said. He kissed her cheek and ran down the steps.

Libby called to her sisters and flew into the house. "Kitty, I need you to find me everything you can about Dutch oven and campfire cookery. Maggie, I need you to come with me and show me what kinds of clothes to pack for a week outdoors." Ranch life had taught the sisters to be calm and quick in a crisis, so the younger girls hopped to do her bidding immediately and without fuss.

Maggie was the tomboy of the family, and she practically lived outdoors. She quickly sifted through Libby, Anne, and Kitty's possessions to assemble an appropriate wardrobe for the week. Libby packed her toiletries and added a few personal touches to the items Maggie had gathered. She gave her sisters instructions on what to do in her absence and kissed them goodbye. Forty five minutes after she found out she was going camping, she was ready to go, and then they were faced with another problem.

In order to have enough horses for the campers, they had appropriated every last horse on the ranch, including Maggie's pony. Hank had been set to bring his own horse, and the mule was too loaded down to take a passenger. As if it were the most natural thing in the world, Dobbie put down his hand to Libby, she swung up into the saddle in front of him, and they were off.

Libby dug in the saddlebag. Pulling out a small bottle, she applied sunscreen to her face and arms. Before he could ask what she was doing she turned and did the same to Dobbie.

"Libby, cowboys don't wear sunscreen," he said.

"And that's why cowboys don't live past forty," she said. He would have protested further, but she was rubbing the lotion gently onto his face, and he lost his train of thought.

At first he kept up a lively conversation for the tourists, but after a while people became absorbed in the beauty of the landscape, so he stopped talking. Once again the gentle lulling of the horse made Libby drowsy, and she fought to keep her eyes open.

Dobbie put his hand on her waist and pulled her back to lean against his chest. "Go to sleep, Sweetheart. I know you're exhausted."

"You are too," she said. He had also been working all hours to get everything ready, and his part in the trip was much larger than hers.

"Maybe I'll go to sleep, too. They're all behind us. Who would know?"

She smiled. Of course he was teasing; he was the only one who knew where they were going. That was her last conscious thought until Dobbie woke her two hours later.

"Libby," he whispered very close to her ear. "It's your turn."

She dismounted from the horse and immediately understood his meaning because ten pairs of eyes were now looking at her as if she were the expert in country food. She knew now what it meant to be "on," and hoped the smile she adopted was charming. It was an easy food day because everything was still fresh, and she had packed a sumptuous feast that morning.

"I hope you all like beef, because that's what we have most of on a cattle ranch. Try not to picture their faces and you'll do all right." That got a chuckle and she made her way around the small circle, talking to people and passing out their lunches. It was a simple sandwich of roast beef and goat cheese on homemade bread. Several people exclaimed over it, and she was thankful she had at least one good meal under her belt. Maybe it would help to smooth over her learning curve as she struggled to cook over a campfire for the first time.

Dobbie claimed a lunch and sat down beside her.

"This is my favorite sandwich," he said.

"Is it?" she asked with mock innocence. She knew very well what his food preferences were, down to how he took his coffee and which jam he liked to spread on his toast. He realized she knew and had made it especially for him. He gave her a warm smile and clasped her hand.

"Miss Libby," a nearby woman said, and Libby startled at the title. It was strange an older person was calling her "Miss," but she realized these people viewed her as their leader, along with Dobbie. "Your sweater is beautiful," the woman continued. "Wherever did you find it?"

"Thank you so much, but I made it," Libby said.

"You made it," the woman repeated with obvious surprise. She reached out and touched the edge of the short sleeve. "It's cashmere. Where on earth did you get cashmere in the middle of Montana?"

"I raise it, and then I can dye it to any color I want. I have a few of these sweaters, and some with long sleeves, too."

"Do you ever sell them?" the woman named Dottie asked.

"Yes, of course," Libby said loudly enough for the rest of the group to hear. "Although, custom orders take a little longer because I have to dye the wool especially for each garment."

An interested murmur rippled through the group.

"How much do you charge?" a man in the back asked.

"Usually a hundred and fifty dollars, but for you folks I'll knock it down to a hundred. Anyone who is interested can sign up when we get back home."

They finished their lunches, and Dobbie helped her up onto the horse. "You usually charge a hundred and fifty?" he whispered, his stubbly whiskers tickling her ear.

"I would if I had ever sold one before."

"You're going to be a millionaire by twenty five, Lib," he said, his tone a mixture of amusement and pride.

"That's the plan," she said.

"I'm not sure about that," he said. "You could be on your way if you had accepted Marcus's proposal."

"I don't want to *marry* a millionaire. I want to *become* a millionaire."

"You looked like you were reconsidering yesterday." He tried and failed to keep his tone casual and disinterested.

"He wants to get back together," she said.

"Do you?"

"He's letting me think about it for a week."

"But do you want to?" he pressed.

"It's pointless to get back in a relationship with him when I'm leaving for college in a few weeks," she said.

"But do you want to, Libby?" he asked with more intensity.

"I...I'm very confused right now, Dobbie."

He didn't say anything, but tension poured off him as he held himself rigidly behind her. She lightly stroked his forearm with her hand until she felt him relax. He took her hand and laced their fingers together.

"You look pretty, sweetheart, like a little wildflower. Are these yours?" He tapped her canvas pants with his thumb.

"Yes. I own some pants, just not jeans."

"I never would have guessed you owned cowboy boots; although, if I had I would have guessed they would be red."

She smiled but didn't reply. Marcus had bought her the pretty red boots for Christmas. She had worn them a few times with skirts, but she never imagined she would ever use them for their intended purpose, as she was now.

She pulled out the information on campfire cooking and started to read.

"You look like Kitty," Dobbie said. "I thought she was the only one who read while riding a horse."

"Kitty found this for me."

"What is it?"

"Information about how to cook over a campfire."

He paused while he thought that over. To him cooking over a campfire involved lighting the fire and cooking the food until it was done, but it never tasted very good. He supposed Libby knew there was an art to cooking it properly and making sure it wasn't burned. Maybe her reluctance to come on the trip had less to do with her fear of wildlife and more to do with her fear of failure.

"I think you're going to do great, Libby, but if not then we'll tell them we eat our food burned in Montana."

She laughed and the tension eased out of her. "Thanks, Dobbie." She continued to pour over the research, and by the time they arrived at their campsite, she at least had a rudimentary understanding of how to do it. Dobbie started the fire for her, and she noticed a large stack of firewood piled near the camp. Obviously he had gone ahead to prepare each of their sites, and the realization made warmth spread through her. Dobbie was in charge, and he knew exactly what he was doing. She watched him with pride as he instructed the campers on how to unsaddle their horses and rub them down with grass. He was so capable for someone so young. He could do anything, and do it well. He felt her eyes on him and turned to give her a look that made her blush and turn away. When she raised her eyes, she saw several people observing them, and knew they were being watched for any signs of romance. She suppressed a sigh. Now not only did she and Dobbie have to worry about their own turmoil over their relationship, but their campers were most likely observing and discussing them, too. It could turn out to be a very long week.

CHAPTER 11

When the fire was hot, Libby set about making smothered fried chicken with mashed potatoes and gravy. She had packed her fresh ingredients in cooler packs, and they had enough coolness to keep their breakfast ingredients safe. After that, she would have to depend on non-perishable items, as well as what they found along the way. Dobbie planned a day of fishing, but she had to have a backup plan in case no one caught anything.

The pan required constant care as she moved the chicken around to different hot spots. It was hot, heavy work, and she thanked the Lord for her electricity-filled kitchen as she mashed potatoes by hand. She had prepared a dessert of cupcakes the day before, and she was glad she had one less thing to worry about.

The meal was delicious. She was ecstatic with her first success, but realistic over the fact it would get harder from here. She cleaned up in the fading light while Dobbie packed their food in a plastic tarp and hoisted it in a large tree a few dozen yards from the campsite.

Everyone settled their bedrolls around the fire, and Dobbie began to tell them stories. Libby had no idea Dobbie knew any stories, and he had a talent for the telling. The stories ended and everyone lay quietly watching the moon, which was almost full now. Far away a wolf howled and people exclaimed excitedly, but Libby's heart picked up its pace in fear, until Dobbie reached out his hand and grasped hers. A few minutes later she was asleep.

Breakfast the next morning was another easy affair. She scrambled eggs with cheese and served biscotti she had made before leaving home. The coffee was tricky, but after a test batch she got the hang of it. The biscotti were studded with walnuts and dried huckleberries. The huckleberries had cost a king's ransom, but they were almost a rite of passage for tourists in the northwest, and so it had to be done.

"Will we have the opportunity to pick huckleberries?" Dottie asked. She was the most curious and outspoken of the group.

"Huckleberry season isn't until August," Dobbie said. "And where you find huckleberries, you find grizzlies, so, no, we probably won't pick huckleberries."

A disappointed murmur rounded the group and Libby thought again of Mr. Smith's words about the huckleberries.

After a leisurely breakfast and cleanup, Dobbie helped everyone saddle their horses and they were off. Libby was glad she wasn't the only one who was sore this morning, and she knew their pace would be leisurely.

"I didn't know you could tell stories like that," she said softly as she leaned against Dobbie's chest.

"We're both learning things about each other lately," he said as softly, his breath warm against her ear.

"What are you learning about me?"

He paused, unsure how to answer. He was learning there was more to her than he had ever realized. He was learning she was grit and steel and downy softness all rolled into one. He was learning she was what home felt like. "Not as much as I would like to," he said at last, smoothing his thumb up and down her waist a few times until someone caught his attention with a question.

For lunch she made egg salad sandwiches with eggs she had boiled that morning. She was thankful mayonnaise came in hermetically sealed packages now that didn't need to be kept refrigerated. She also set out potato chips, which were slightly crushed, as well as apples and some cookies she had made before their departure. Dobbie disappeared for a while, and when he returned he was carrying four dead rabbits.

"How did you do that?" she asked with a little bit of awe.

"I set live traps ahead of time and killed them just now. I'll skin them for you when we make camp."

She stood on her toes to kiss his cheek. "You're amazing"

Now it was his turn to blush slightly. Once again the others were watching them as if trying to interpret their relationship, but she didn't care. Tonight they would have rabbit, and it would help vary her menu of canned fish, chicken, beef, and venison. Maybe with more surprises like this she might be able to pull off this week as a culinary success.

For the next few hours until supper she planned her meal, and she almost felt like a real pioneer living off the land. They would have her father's favorite rabbit stew over rice, along with a fresh salad of wild greens. To her further delight, they camped near a large blackberry patch, and she immediately decided to make a skillet cobbler.

The resulting meal was better than she could have hoped, and she thought maybe an open fire had some magical ability to make even simple food taste better. The group complimented her on the cuisine, even those who had been reluctant to taste rabbit.

"Have you ever considered putting out a cookbook?" This, of course, came from Dottie.

"Why, yes, as a matter of fact I do have a cookbook." She had anticipated the question and prepared a cookbook of regional favorites as well as all the recipes she had planned for Hank to use. "This recipe isn't in it, but my email address is in the back of the book, and I would be glad to send it to you."

Dobbie coughed, and it sounded suspiciously like a laugh.

Later he leaned over to whisper in her ear. "Did you bring a camera so you can take pictures and then sell them those?"

"No, but that's a wonderful idea."

When he realized she was serious, he laughed again. "I'm surprised you're not going to try and sell me to the highest bidder."

"Who says I'm not?" she asked, and dodged him when he tried to pinch her waist.

His amusement increased when in the morning she made scones and set out jars of jam with her own label.

"Let me guess, these are available for purchase," he said only loudly enough for her to hear, and this time he had to dodge her as she attempted to poke him.

That day they only rode for a little while, made camp, and spent the afternoon fishing. Dobbie gave those who wanted to learn a lesson in basic pole construction and fishing. Two brothers had brought their fly-fishing equipment, and a fierce competition developed to see who could catch the most fish—the fly-fishermen or those with homemade poles.

In the end the fly-fishermen won, but not by a large margin. Everyone was laughing and happy, and Libby kept busy frying up batches of trout and potatoes. For dessert she made a skillet apple pie, and it was eaten so quickly she had to make another.

After supper, Dobbie asked her to tell some stories about her wild uncle Bill. He had been her grandfather's brother, and she only had vague memories of him, but the stories were legendary. He lived in the woods and only came inside for Christmas and Easter. He had a wolf for a dog and hated grizzly bears for a reason no one ever knew. It was rumored he once wrestled an adult male grizzly bear and won, but Libby thought that was probably a myth.

"What did he die of?" someone asked.

"Skin cancer," Libby said, with a significant look to Dobbie who rolled his eyes.

The next morning Libby baked raisin bread for breakfast and iced it with a powdered sugar glaze. She had made the dough the previous night and left it to rise overnight. It was such a hit she made more dough without raisins and set it to rise for that evening's meal. That night they had venison stew made from meat she had canned the previous fall. Most of the tourists were city dwellers and had never tasted wild game before. She guessed correctly that, at the very least, they would enjoy the adventure of trying something they could tell their friends at home about.

She was amused by their comments about how idyllic her life was, and then her amusement turned to contemplation. Was her life idyllic? It was certainly a lot of work. She thought of the many hours she had put in harvesting and canning the food they were now eating, but it had been rewarding and enjoyable.

She sat back to study the people around her. They had what she dreamed of. Most of them were wealthy and cultured city folk. A few were from Washington DC, three were from New York, and yet they wanted what she had. Why? Was it because the grass was always greener someplace else, or was it because her life was, as they said, idyllic?

It was an interesting thought. For so long now she had been intent on escape, but to what end? Where did she want to go? What did she really want? She had never asked herself that question before.

"You're quiet," Dobbie said the next day when they were on his horse. They had spent their time together talking the last few days.

"Where did you go when you went away?" she asked.

"A little bit of everywhere. I worked ranches in Wyoming, New Mexico, and Texas."

"What was it like?"

"The same as here. Lots of land, lots of cows."

"Why did you come back?"

He thought that over for a while before he answered. "The people were all the same everywhere I went. Some were mean, and some were nice. Some were stingy, and some were giving. Some were crazy, and others were boring. Here's what I realized, though: they weren't my people. You, and your sisters, and your dad are my family. I belong to you, and you belong to me, and belonging makes all the difference."

She thought that through. What would it be like to live somewhere and be alone? To not have anyone to take care of you and, worse, to not have anyone to take care of? She shivered. It was a lonely, scary thought.

"Lots of people go away," she said. "It doesn't mean you stop belonging to each other."

"True, but only if you have the intention of coming back. Otherwise you meet new people and make a new life for yourself where you are."

His words made her think of Anne. Anne went away, but Anne had Will and his family. She was also making new friends in Pittsburgh where she now lived. When Libby went away to Omaha, she would be all alone until she made new friends. How long would that take? Suddenly the prospect of leaving didn't sound nearly as enticing, and she snuggled closer to Dobbie's powerful chest. In response, he wrapped both arms around her and hugged her tightly and kissed her cheek. And at this moment, there was nowhere else she would rather be.

CHAPTER 12

The next day they woke to rain. It hadn't rained all week, so they were lucky, but it still made for a miserable ride. Dobbie had provided everyone with plastic ponchos, so they pulled them out and put them on. He didn't have one for Libby because Hank had planned to bring his own, so he and Libby shared his after she made a larger opening for their faces. The rain and wind made it feel cold. Libby edged closer to Dobbie's warmth, and he cinched his arms more tightly around her.

"We fit together perfectly," he said, and it surprised her he would say out loud what she had been thinking.

"We do," she agreed. Her favorite part of the trip was quickly becoming the time they spent in the saddle because it was also time spent in his arms.

"It feels like we're in our own world with the rain beating down around us in sheets, blocking out all the other sights and sounds," he said. He kissed the rim of her ear, and she shivered. "Cold, baby?"

She shook her head. "Tell me a story," she pled. She loved to hear him tell stories at the campfire each night. He had an unexpected talent for it, and she sat mesmerized along with the other campers.

"Once there were four princesses. Each was beautiful in her own way, and each was different from the others. Their father held a vast kingdom, and one day a neighboring knight came to claim one of the princesses for his bride. The king told him he would have to take the oldest daughter because the daughters had to be married in order. The knight was happy because he liked the oldest daughter. She was strong and brave, like him, and they liked to joust together and have swordfights.

"One day he was walking across the battlefield, thinking of his bride to be, when he saw a beautiful maiden, the most beautiful maiden in all the land. She was so wondrous he stopped and stared at her, awed any woman could be so lovely. She turned haughty eyes to him and told him his armor was in need of polishing, and then she put up her nose and walked away.

"The knight tried to forget her, but he couldn't. He was angry she had made fun of his armor, and he became obsessed with paying her back, but first he had to find out who she was. He spied on the royal court for days until he learned she was the second daughter of the king. She was nothing like her sister. She didn't like jousting or sword fighting. She liked to read and sew and sit with her handmaidens talking about girlish things. He tried to feel contempt for her, but he couldn't, and he soon realized she was the true princess of his heart, and she was the one he wanted.

"He faced a dilemma, though. He liked the older daughter, and didn't want to break her heart. If he betrayed her, the king would surely have his head. And every time he saw the second daughter she seemed to hate him more. Once she threw a battle axe at him, which was strange because to everyone else she was sweet and loving."

Libby smiled, but hid it when he continued.

"The knight decided to seek advice from a wise man who was traveling through the countryside. The wise man was puny and weak, but he was not without merit. When the knight told the wise man of the great beauty of the older sister, he asked to be taken to her that he might meet her. The knight took the wise man and introduced him to his bride, and knew right away his problem had been solved. The wise man took one look at the oldest daughter and immediately fell in love with her. She fell in love with him, although she wasn't used to feeling love, and had to be shown how to use her emotions without applying her sword. They married and the knight was free to pursue the second daughter.

"But there was a problem: The second daughter still thought she didn't want the knight. She dreamed of going to a foreign country where the men played harps all day and ate stinky cheese. She had never been to this country, but she thought it might be nice to live somewhere else for a change. The knight tried to convince her all countries were the same, and he was the knight for her."

He stopped talking. Libby didn't realize how intently she had been listening until he stopped speaking.

"What did she do? How did it end?" she asked.

"You tell me," he said. "You make up the ending for this one."

She swallowed hard, and thought fast. "The knight realized if he truly cared about her, he had to let her go, but he promised to wait for her while she was gone exploring."

"And did she come back to him?" he asked.

"She's still exploring, but she has the hope that somehow, someway they'll someday be together," she said.

She didn't realize how tense she was until he smoothed his thumb over her waist, and she began to relax.

"He's a patient knight," he said.

"It's his turn to be patient. She was patient while he was gone exploring for two years."

He smiled. "I don't remember that part being in the story."

"I'm pretty sure you mentioned that the knight went away for two long, miserable years," she said.

He chuckled, and they moved on to another topic.

By the time they arrived at the campsite it had stopped raining, but everyone was damp and uncomfortable. They wandered off into the woods to change their clothes, but Dobbie captured Libby's hand and led her behind him into the woods. They walked for a little way until they reached the mountain. They had been skirting the edge of the mountain the entire trip, and running parallel with its stream. Now they stepped into a clearing and Dobbie pointed.

The massive amount of rain had created a small waterfall, which was now tumbling over a craggy ridge in the mountain. Dobbie opened his hand and revealed her shampoo.

Libby gasped. Her hair felt grimy and greasy, but the possibility of washing it had never occurred to her, even though she had brought all her toiletries in case.

"Will you come with me?" she asked. It was across the stream, and she was afraid of snakes.

In answer, he tucked her hand in his again and led the way. He picked his way across the stream and carried her over the deepest parts. He deposited her near the waterfall. She stuck her head under the trickle of water, and when it was thoroughly wet, she lathered it and started to rinse. It felt like heaven to be clean, even if it was only her hair. She washed her face and felt her hair to make sure the soap was out. It wasn't, and she couldn't make the small spray of water reach where she wanted.

"Dobbie, will you help me rinse?" she asked.

He turned to her with a helpless look. "I don't know how to do girl stuff," he said.

"You know how to rinse soap out of hair, surely. It's not that difficult. I can't make the water reach it because I can't see where it's going. Please?"

He reached his arms around her to gently tilt her head in the direction of the water and used his hands to work the soap out of her hair. She closed her eyes and enjoyed the sensation of his fingers in her hair, but then all too soon it was over.

"Your turn?" She opened her eyes and held out her shampoo to him.

He grimaced. "I'll smell girly."

"I'm the only one who is close enough to smell you every day, and I don't mind," she said.

He eyed the shampoo. "Are you going to help me?" His gaze met hers, and she felt a jolt of electricity all the way to the soles of her feet.

"Yes," she whispered; although, she didn't know why she was whispering. He took off his Stetson and set it on a rock. She stood on her toes to lather his hair, and now it was his turn to close his eyes. She directed his head under the stream and used her hands to work out the lather.

"There," she proclaimed when all the shampoo was out of his hair.

He opened his eyes and caught her hand. Slowly and purposefully he brought her hand to his face, kissed the inside of her wrist, and gently and slowly made his way up to the tender inside of her elbow. She watched him with rapt attention and felt herself being drawn into the spell he was weaving.

"We should get back to our campers." He said it softly. She nodded, though she had no idea what he said.

He grinned at her, amused by her besotted state. "Libby, honey, we're going to have to go. Are your legs working all right?"

That registered. She picked up his Stetson and jammed it on his head.

"You love to tease me, don't you, Shane?" she asked.

"Yes," he said seriously. "But so far I haven't found anything I don't love to do with you." He picked her up and carried her over the stream. Then he took her hand and led her dazzled and speechless back to the campsite.

CHAPTER 13

*L*ibby couldn't believe the trip was already half over, especially when she realized she was having more fun than she remembered in recent history. Not having spent much time outdoors, she was as new to the scenery as the tourists. She found herself sharing the enjoyment and wonder over every beautiful sunset, bird, or mountain vista.

When they turned around, Dobbie led them back a different way than they came, so it seemed like a whole new trip. If she was enjoying the scenery, she was in awe of Dobbie. She knew he was good at his job as ranch foreman, but she had no idea he had so much mastery in so many different areas. He was so *capable*. Nothing upset him, nothing caught him off guard, and he could seemingly do everything.

One day, their first day heading back, Dobbie held up his hand for the horses to stop. They had been riding single file on an elk path through heavy brush. Libby didn't see what the problem was until he pulled out his revolver, moved her aside with one arm, and told her to cover her ears. She did, then saw the rattlesnake's body fly through the air and land in a heap two feet in front of their horse.

"I hate to do that," he said regretfully. "But there was no getting around it, and they scare the horses." He waited a few minutes until the snake's body stopped convulsing, and then he urged his horse on.

Libby turned her head and watched him for a long time as those behind them exclaimed over the snake. There was real fear in their voices, but for Dobbie it was an everyday occurrence, and she sensed how special he really was. He was a relic, a throwback, and the last of a dying breed of men who faced danger head on with protecting their loved ones as their only thought. For some reason she was picturing him as a soldier. He would be a leader in war, she was certain.

"Looking at me like that will get you kissed," he said, and she turned and faced forward with a smile. She never would have guessed he had such a soft, tender side. How many men were so strong, and yet so gentle? It was a rare combination, and she wondered if it made him the perfect man. Or maybe her perfect man. How could a camping trip stir so many deep thoughts for her?

The next evening when everyone was settled in their beds, he held out his hand to her and led her stealthily behind him into the woods.

"I want to show you something I found," he whispered. He led her to a small lean-to. It was crudely constructed, and Libby remembered seeing Maggie and Mathew Henshaw carrying a load of old boards into the woods a few years ago.

"Maggie built this," she said. "But this isn't far from the house. Will we be home tomorrow?"

He shook his head. "We're taking a circuitous route that weaves in and out. Tomorrow we'll head back out before going home again." He nodded toward the tiny structure. "Look." He pointed to the side of the fort where Maggie and Matthew's initials were carved, along with Anne and Will's. Dobbie tapped the panel beside Anne and Will's initials, and she turned her gaze to see, "E.C and S.D."

She gasped. "When did you do that?"

"When I found this place as I was staking out the camping trip a couple of weeks ago." He took her hand, wound their fingers together, and they stared at the initials for a few minutes. She wondered if it bothered him to see Anne and Will's initials there together, but reasoned it must not if he carved theirs beside them.

"What if someone sees?" she asked.

"What if they do? I have feelings for you, and I don't care if people know it."

She turned to face him. The electricity between them was immediate and intense, but neither of them felt like a makeout session would be in the best interest of the mature and responsible image they were trying to cultivate for their campers. Dobbie let out a frustrated sigh.

"Sometimes I get really tired of being a grownup, Libby," he said.

Sometimes she did, too. She felt like they had both been adults forever. Would it ever be their turn to be kids? "I'll race you back to camp." She turned and ran off with a giggle, and he grinned as he followed behind her.

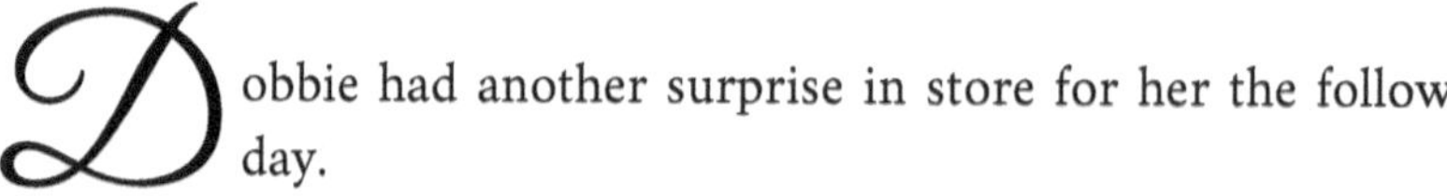

*D*obbie had another surprise in store for her the following day.

"Skeet," Dottie announced as they came into the clearing where they would make camp that night.

Libby gave Dobbie a questioning glance. There was a clay pigeon launcher in the middle of the meadow. "How did you get this here?"

"Very carefully," he replied, grinning because he had pulled one over on her. He possessed the only shotgun in the group, so those who wanted to participate had to take turns. But his ammo supply was plentiful, and no one minded the wait. In fact, everyone seemed to be having a delightful time watching each other shoot.

Libby bustled around preparing supper and not paying much attention until she heard Dobbie call her name. "Your turn, Lib."

She looked up in astonishment, ready to refuse. But to her chagrin, she found everyone staring at her expectantly.

"I don't know how to shoot skeet," she replied, hating to disappoint the group. They were probably under the impression all Montana girls were born with guns in their hands.

"Neither did anyone else until today," Dobbie said reasonably. "Give it a try."

She wanted to refuse but had no idea how without being a wet blanket. Instead, she wrinkled her nose at Dobbie who was wearing a Cheshire-cat grin. He knew he had her pinned, and he was enjoying her discomfort. He instructed her on how to aim and when to fire.

"He didn't put his arms around *me* when he was telling me what to do." This came from Dottie's cousin. She was sixty with a wry sense of humor.

Dobbie chuckled softly, very close to Libby's ear. She hadn't been paying attention when he was instructing the other shooters, so she had no idea he hadn't wrapped both arms tightly about them as he had with her. A scarlet blush stole up her cheeks, and she willed it away.

"Tell me when you're ready." He let her go and stepped back.

Nervously, she licked her lips and tried to focus on the spot where she guessed the clay pigeon would soon be. "Pull," she commanded. There was a whirring sound, then whizzing, and then she saw the pigeon. It was much larger than she was expecting it to be, and moving slowly, but she still had no illusions about her ability to hit it.

She pulled the trigger, forgetting to brace it on her shoulder the way Dobbie showed her. The fierce kickback knocked her to the ground, momentarily stunning her as she landed hard on her behind.

"Oh," she said in consternation. There had been no sound signaling the explosion of the clay disc. She bit her lip, stifling her disappointment. Maybe the humiliation of being knocked over would have been worth it if only she had hit her target.

It took her a minute to realize the rest of the group was exclaiming in wonder over something in the distance. "You hit it," one of the men said. "I can't believe you hit it!"

"But I didn't," she protested. No one listened to her. They were laughing and chatting excitedly until at last the same man who had spoken ran a few dozen yards into the distance. He returned holding a dead mallard upside down in his hand.

"I killed a duck?" she exclaimed.

The group laughed at her bewildered expression. For the rest of the evening, they called her "Deadeye." She tried to enjoy their hilarity, but something about the situation bothered her.

That night when she lay by the fire, she could no longer contain her emotions and began to sniffle.

Dobbie sat up in alarm, trying to see her by the dim firelight. "Libby, are you afraid?"

She shook her head before remembering he couldn't see her. "No." Her voice was tremulous. She swiped impatiently at her tears.

Quietly, so as not to draw attention to them, he scooted over to her bedroll. "What is it, Sweetheart? Don't tell me the teasing hurt your feelings tonight." He put his arm around her. She pressed her face to his chest and shook her head.

"Then what is it? Please tell me."

"Mallards mate for life," she said. "I widowed a duck." Unable to contain her tears any longer, she pressed her face to his chest and cried. Drat Kitty and her fountain of knowledge. Without her brainy little sister, Libby would never have known such useless trivia.

Dobbie made a choking sound and didn't speak for a long time. He ran his hand soothingly down her back. At last he spoke. "That duck was flying alone. He was probably a teenager who hadn't taken a mate yet." He made the choking sound again and coughed.

"You really think so?" she whispered. She raised her head a notch to study his expression.

He nodded emphatically. "And even if you did widow some poor female, she can always find another mate." She rested her head on his shoulder and he played absently with her hair.

"My dad didn't," she said.

He didn't tease her for her leap in logic. Instead, he became serious, too. "I wouldn't, either. If something happened to the woman I had pledged my life to, I wouldn't go looking for another."

She was quiet, processing that. "Poor duck." Her voice trembled again but the way he was gently running his fingers through her hair was very soothing. He coughed again. Briefly, she wondered if he was laughing at her, but sleep overtook her before she could find out.

CHAPTER 14

The following days of their journey passed quickly and pleasantly. Libby felt grimy because she hadn't bathed in nearly a week, but everyone else was in the same state, and she found she minded less than she thought she would.

The rest of the meals went off without a hitch. The only problem was that she had saved s'mores as dessert for their last supper. The chocolate was soft and gooey, and the marshmallows had formed into one giant gob, but Dobbie made a joke of cutting them into cubes with his knife, and no one seemed to mind.

The next morning, their last, Libby made cinnamon rolls. She finished cleaning the last pan when she heard a heart-stopping sound come from the bushes. If she lived to a hundred, she knew she would never forget the sound of that pain-filled scream and, worst of all, she knew it came from Dobbie.

She followed the sound with her heart in her throat, certain he had been attacked by a bear. She grabbed a stick as she ran, determined to chase it away. If she had to, she would beat it off or die trying.

But when she reached him, there was no bear; there was only Dobbie lying motionless and colorless on the forest floor. At first she thought he must have shot himself by accident, but she hadn't heard a shot, and there was no blood. And then she saw it. There attached to his leg was one of her Uncle Bill's very old and very illegal bear traps.

It surrounded the middle of his calf like a large rusty set of teeth. The metal points were a few inches long, and they were imbedded so far in his flesh they were invisible. First she knelt beside him and felt for a pulse. He was alive, but he was unconscious. *Shock.* The thought came from some unknown part of her brain, but she knew shock could be as dangerous as blood loss, which was her next concern. He wasn't bleeding, but as soon as she removed the trap from his leg he was going to gush.

She forced her mind to calm down and think what to do. If the trap had hit an artery and she took it off, he would bleed to death. Were there major arteries in the lower leg? She knew about the one in the thigh from a cowboy who had been gored by one of their bulls. She didn't think the lower leg was as risky as the upper thigh, but she wasn't sure.

One thing she knew: If she didn't take off the trap, Dobbie would lose his lower leg for sure. She decided to risk it. Knowing him, he would rather be dead than missing a limb, painful though that thought was. Her father had one of these traps as a keepsake, and he had once showed her how it worked. It was heavy and rusty, but her adrenaline made her strong, and so she pried it apart. When she did, Dobbie moaned, and blood began to pour from his wounds. She prayed she hadn't done the wrong thing and signed his death sentence. The blood was pulsing out now, and it became her new number one priority.

She heard a sound behind her and turned to find all the campers watching her with wide, scared eyes.

"Go to his horse and retrieve the first aid kit," she directed one of the men. She described it to him and sent him on his way. She surveyed the rest of them. "Does anyone know anything about plants?"

Dottie, bless her, raised her hand.

"Do you know what wild yarrow looks like?" she asked and Dottie nodded. "There was a large clump on the other side of the trail. Gather as much as you can." Libby would never again complain about Kitty's constant spouting of information. Only a couple of months ago she had told them Achilles used wild yarrow to staunch the blood of his soldiers' wounds.

The man whose name she couldn't remember returned with the first aid kit. Libby cut off the bottom half of Dobbie's pant leg and had to swallow down her nausea. His leg was scarlet with blood. She poured water over it until she could see the leg and then gently swiped it with antibacterial wipes while Dobbie moaned and tried to thrash around. He was starting to come to, but she didn't want him to. She gave him some sleep aid he sometimes took for his insomnia and hoped it would help. Dottie returned with the yarrow. Libby had no idea how to use it, so she pressed both flowers and stems against his leg and then wrapped it in a bandage.

"Go saddle your horses," she said, and tried to keep the strain out of her voice. She held back the two largest men, and they carried Dobbie back to camp.

Everyone stood around looking to her for direction, and she had to resist the urge not to panic and flee back into the woods. She had no idea where they were, and no idea how to get back home.

Instead, she remained calm and smiled at everyone before going around to check each of their saddles, the same way Dobbie did every morning before they set off. She hadn't saddled a horse in years, and she tried hard to remember everything her father had taught her. She punched a few flanks and tightened a few cinches, but otherwise the campers had done well.

"I need two volunteers to ride together today," she said. Dottie and another older woman raised their hands. Libby appropriated Maggie's pony, pinned a note to her saddle blanket, and then slapped her behind with the instruction to, "Find Maggie." The pony took off at a run, and Libby watched her go with a hopeless, scared expression before plastering the confident smile back on her face. She turned to the group.

"And now we ride," she said pleasantly. She climbed into the saddle of Dobbie's horse and waited while the other men hoisted Dobbie into the saddle behind her. She wrapped his arms around her waist so he was slumped forward against her back, and then she took off.

The problem was that she had no idea where she was going. She gave the horse its head with the instruction to go home, and then she prayed he would lead them there and not a field of sweet grass or a cool stream.

She did a lot of praying on that trip because it was all she could do.

At lunch she set out peanut butter, jam, and bread with apologies, but no one seemed to mind. She coaxed Dobbie to drink some water, changed his bandage, and applied more yarrow.

The bleeding had subsided, and she took that as a good sign that no arteries had been nicked. Dobbie was still out, and she didn't know if he was unconscious or merely asleep.

The hours after lunch seemed endless. She was beginning to lose faith in the horse when familiar landmarks came into view, and she saw her house in the distance. She wanted to burst into tears and urge her horse to a run, but she remained calm and cheerful as she told the campers their ride was almost over and they would all be able to shower and sleep in a real bed soon.

They reached the house, and she saw the sweetest sight she had ever witnessed. Maggie's pony had reached home with her message and the Henshaw's helicopter was parked on their lawn. It was a fifty-minute drive to the Henshaw's, and so she had sent the pony ahead to have the helicopter ready for their arrival because the nearest hospital was hours away by car.

She greeted Maggie and Kitty with a reminder to keep their tears at bay, and do their duty, and then she turned to her campers.

"I would love to say a proper goodbye to you all, as I know Dobbie would, but I'm going to see him to the hospital now. My sisters and our ranch hands will see you off. Farewell."

She shouldn't have been surprised to learn Marcus was piloting the helicopter, but she still was. He and a couple of their hands settled Dobbie in the back of the aircraft. It had been altered to allow for livestock, so there were two seats in the front and a cavern-like opening in the back.

Libby climbed in the back and held tightly to Dobbie so he wouldn't shift around. She waited until the sound of the engine would drown out her tears, and then she gave way to her weeping.

Her tears must have roused Dobbie because his eyes became slits and he squinted at her. "Libby, am I dying? Is that why you're crying?" The corners of his mouth turned up slightly in the hint of a smile.

"No, I'm afraid of flying, and your blood is making a mess everywhere."

He smiled wider now. "My girl." His hand reached to the back of her head and pulled her forward. They kissed softly and tenderly until he slipped back into unconsciousness.

She thought the helicopter was her breaking point until they reached the hospital and nurses took him away from her, and then she became hysterical.

Marcus picked her up around the waist and half carried, half dragged her to the waiting room. He sat beside her and tried to soothe her while they waited. Her hysteria subsided into weeping, and she buried her face in his shoulder.

After what seemed an eternity the doctor emerged.

"Are you the one who used the yarrow?" was his first question. When she answered yes, he grunted, and she couldn't tell if it was approval or disapproval.

"He's going to be fine. The puncture wounds were deep, but clean, so no stitches. He has a small fracture from the force of the trap, and he lost a lot of blood. We've loaded him up on painkillers and antibiotics, but he'll need to stay off his feet for a little while."

Libby nodded. That wouldn't be easy to accomplish, but she would tie him down if she had to. Knowing Dobbie she might have to.

"When can I see him?" she asked.

"We'll keep him overnight for observation, and you can take him home tomorrow. When the wounds heal we might have to put him in an air cast, but we'll cross that bridge when we get to it."

She nodded and followed him to Dobbie's room while Marcus waited in the lobby. The doctor didn't go in with her, so she pushed open the door and stood for a minute looking at him. She had never seen him in anything but shirts and jeans, and to see him in a hospital gown was startling. He looked vulnerable, like he had after the fire when he was a boy, although now he rippled with powerful muscles that a thin gown couldn't veil.

She approached the edge of the bed and took his hand. She leaned forward to press a gentle kiss to his forehead and then lost control completely, raining gentle kisses all over his face. Somewhere in the middle of that he woke up and tried to kiss her in return, but his muscles wouldn't cooperate the way he wanted. She pulled back to look at him. He tried to smile, but only half his mouth was working because of the powerful pain killers they had given him.

"Ibby," he said. "Ove oo." And then he was out again.

Libby froze. What had he said? Was he trying to tell her he loved her? She brushed the thought aside. It was no matter. A man's drug-induced confession couldn't be held against him.

After satisfying herself he was all right, she went back to the lobby and to Marcus. He held out his cell phone to her. She didn't own one because their ranch had no reception, but Marcus's family installed a tower for their own use and all the hands communicated with each other by cell phones. She called Kitty, and filled her in on the situation, then handed the phone back to Marcus.

"Thank you," she said sincerely. "For everything."

He smiled, a little sadly, she thought. "You and Dobbie. Wow. I did not see that coming."

She blushed three shades of crimson. "We're friends," she insisted.

He raised an eyebrow at her.

"I'm going to college in the fall."

"Are you really?" he asked.

She let out a breath she didn't know she'd been holding. "I'm sorry, Marcus, that things didn't work out between us. I don't know why they didn't."

"I think he's lying in a hospital bed."

She pinched his arm. "You stop that. You're making me blush."

"I like it when you blush." Now it was his turn to sigh. "You're the perfect ranch wife, Libby. Looks like I'm not the only one who knows it."

He squeezed her hand, stood, and walked away.

CHAPTER 15

*L*ibby went back to Dobbie's room and checked his wallet. She gave a sigh of relief when she found money. She didn't have anything with her except her clothes and lip balm, and she was suddenly famished.

She retrieved a tray from the cafeteria and brought it back to Dobbie's room, but still he slept. She found an extra blanket for herself, curled up in the uncomfortable chair beside his bed, and fell into a dead sleep. Sometime later she was awakened by whimpers and thrashing. She stood over Dobbie's bed and tried to settle him. When she couldn't, she shook him slightly until he opened his eyes to look at her.

"Libby?"

"I'm here, Shane."

"Don't leave me," he pled, and she thought he was probably still asleep. He held out his arms to her. "Please don't leave me."

She leaned over the bed and hugged him tightly while making soft soothing noises by his ear. Finally he quieted down. She tried to ease out of his embrace, but every time he tightened his grip, so she finally crawled in beside him and slept until daybreak when she woke again and went back to the chair.

The next time she woke he was awake and looking at her.

"Hey, little bit," he said with a groggy smile. "Do I look as bad as you?"

She looked down to survey herself and couldn't believe her appearance. Her clothes and hair were matted with his dried blood and, besides that, she was dusty and grimy.

"I'm not sure anyone in history has ever looked this bad," she said.

He held out his hand to her. She went forward to take it and perched on the edge of his bed.

"You scared me." She brushed the hair off his face and smoothed her palm on his cheek.

"Sorry about that. What exactly happened?"

She told him about the bear trap and how she had gotten him home and to the hospital. His hand tightened on hers when she got to the part about Marcus flying them to the hospital.

"And he stayed with you?" he asked.

"For a little while." He gave her a searching gaze, and she dropped her eyes to the blanket because she was afraid to have him see the deep emotion there. "He seems to think we're involved with each other."

"I guess college does make you smart," he said. He picked up her hand and kissed it. "I can't believe you took care of me all on your own and led everyone home. I've never met anyone more capable of anything than you. Did I do or say anything embarrassing while I was under sedation?"

She thought of his possible love confession and his plea for her not to leave him in the night, but she was saved from answering by the appearance of her father. He must have been worried if he came himself, instead of sending one of the ranch hands.

"Hi, Son," he said, and came forward to lay his hand on Dobbie's shoulder. "Sorry about the leg. I thought we had collected all those blasted traps."

Dobbie smiled. "Better me than one of the tourists. Those city types always sue."

They laughed together, and Libby thought how alike they were.

They were both manly men who put duty, honor, and family pride above everything else. Before her mother's death her father had been tender, loving, and involved in their lives, but after he had closeted a part of his heart away. It was as if he didn't know how to be vulnerable without his wife to teach him. She studied Dobbie while the two men talked about the ranch. Could his newfound gentleness be due to her? Was she somehow helping him tap untouched parts of his heart? If she married him, would he be a kind and loving father to their kids, like her father had been?

She shook her head to clear it. Where had that thought come from? Of course she wouldn't marry Dobbie. She was going to go away and marry someone from the city, and Dobbie would…What would Dobbie do?

The thought of Dobbie with another woman was painful on many levels. To think of some other woman loving him and living with him at their ranch evoked a jealousy in her she didn't realize she possessed. Besides that, now that she had realized she brought out his soft, gentle side, she wondered if someone else would affect him the same way. Maybe it was egotistical of her, but she thought she was the only one who was able to get at his vulnerable core. If he were with someone else, would he hide that part of himself away and only present his stable, hard-working side? It was a sad thought, especially when she knew he was capable of so much more.

Both men were now looking at her, and she realized Dobbie was recounting her part in his rescue. Her father was looking at her with equal parts affection and pride, and so was Dobbie.

"You're a sight, little girl," her father said. "Never thought I would see the day when you would be so filthy." He held out a bag to her. "Your sister sent some things."

"Bless her," Libby said. She tore the bag from her father's fingers and sprinted to the bathroom in Dobbie's room. She took a long shower and washed her hair three times. When she emerged wearing one of her feminine dresses and a touch of makeup with her hair perfectly styled, she felt like a whole new person.

"Hey, Beautiful," Dobbie said when she emerged.

She was amazed it sounded so natural, as if he had always talked to her this way. He held open his hand and she took it before perching on the edge of his bed.

"Where's Dad?"

"Trying to spring me, so we should make use of the time while we can." He urged her forward, but before he could kiss her he stopped and inhaled. "Strawberries." He gave her a teasing smile. "With this bandage on, I'm going to need someone to give me a sponge bath."

She smiled mischievously and nuzzled her nose against his cheek. "I'll send Rook."

He groaned and she giggled. Rook was their oldest cowboy, a grizzled, wiry man who barely spoke to anyone.

"How can you be so cruel when I'm suffering so much? I think I need a kiss to make me feel better."

She pulled away slightly so she hovered in front of his face. "Just one?"

"That's more like it," he said, and his hand slid to the back of her head.

"I did it," her father spoke from the doorway, and they jumped guiltily apart. "You're free. Let's get you out of here." He helped get Dobbie dressed while Libby retrieved a wheelchair.

The two-hour car ride home was misery for Dobbie who held his leg stiffly in front of him and tried not to wince with the pain. Libby stopped worrying about her father's watchful eye. She took Dobbie's hand and massaged it gently until he relaxed visibly.

They set him up in Anne's bedroom, which was an irony unto itself, but it was the only available room. Libby made sure he was properly set up and got to work on everything she had missed in her absence. Kitty and Maggie had done an admirable job of keeping the house clean, but her garden needed watered and weeded, supper needed to be made, and laundry was piled a couple of feet high.

She knew Dobbie would be bored and restless, so she sent first Maggie and then Kitty to entertain him. She also encountered Rook on her way to the goat pen, and when she told him what she wanted him to do, he gave her one of his rare toothless smiles. A few minutes later she heard Dobbie thunder her name and Rook's brittle little cackle echoed through the house. He descended the stairs sopping wet, laid the sponge on the counter, and exited the house still laughing.

She didn't have a chance to visit him until supper that night, and he was in a predictably bad mood.

"Look who finally showed up," he said grumpily.

She adjusted the shade because the sun was in his face. "I'm in time for the pity party, I see. Buck up. You're acting like someone who stepped in a bear trap."

"Maggie beat me at chess, checkers, and cards, Kitty read me a book I couldn't understand, and then Rook looked like he enjoyed the prospect of my sponge bath a little too much. So you'd better have brought something good to top all that."

"I brought supper." She revealed his tray with a flourish.

His face lit up but then fell when he only saw one plate and one fork. "You already ate?"

"No," she said and set about feeding him and sharing his meal.

"What are you going to do when you're an old man and can't work fourteen hours every day?" she asked. "You're going to go crazy." She used the napkin to wipe his mouth. Of course he could have done it, but they both pretended it was necessary for her to hover so close to him.

He caught her palm and kissed it. "Maybe by then I'll have other interests to keep me occupied."

She wasn't sure what he meant exactly, but his insinuation, as well as his tone, made her flush. He moved his lips down to her wrist and nibbled at the delicate flesh there so when he tugged her forward, she was too entranced to protest. Before she could reach him, Maggie bounded into the room with her checkerboard. To his credit, he greeted Maggie cheerfully and agreed to play with her.

Libby cleared away the tray while Maggie set up the board, and before she left, she paused in the entryway. She loved the picture he made, sitting up and smiling cheerfully at her sweet little sister. He caught her look, gave her a wink, and she turned to go back to the kitchen.

CHAPTER 16

*L*ibby was able to keep Dobbie bedridden for three days, which was three days more than she had anticipated. On the fourth day, when he insisted he was getting up, she innocently asked him if he would help her return the mule to the Henshaws. Of course she could have sent one of the ranch hands, but she counted on the fact his jealousy over Marcus would make him go with her, and she was correct.

"You're bringing him a pie?" he asked as she shoved it into his hands to hold.

"We owe them much more than a pie, and besides, strawberry is his favorite. He says it reminds him of me for some reason."

That innocent comment made him murderously angry, but not as much as the fact that she insisted on driving.

"I will not be driven by a girl," he said, and started to get out of the truck.

She rested her hand on his leg and he paused. "Your foot can't press the clutch."

"It can," he insisted, despite the fact he was still in a lot of pain. His tone was softer now, though, and he glanced at her hand on his thigh.

Pressing her advantage she crept closer to him. "Shane, if I were injured, is there anything in the world that would keep you from taking care of me?"

"Nothing," he murmured.

"Then why are you trying to stop me? You're making my job harder." Her hand slid up to rest on his chest. "Can't you let me fuss over you a little bit?"

"I suppose." He blinked at her, and his gaze dropped to her lips. They had so little privacy in the house. Even though he'd been with her every day in the house, he missed her, missed the sweet intimacy that had arisen during the campout. He wanted to kiss her again, to see where it might lead. But how could he do that when they were never alone?

Libby was having similar thoughts, though hers were swirled with fear. She both wanted and didn't want him to kiss her again. A part of her was curious, but another part of her understood the closer they grew, the harder it would be to walk away when it was over. And it would have to be over eventually, wouldn't it? Marcus had seemed perfect to her, but their relationship proved unsustainable. If she couldn't make it with Marcus Henshaw, she couldn't make it with Dobbie, could she?

The ride to the Henshaws was silent, each of them lost in dreary thoughts about their future. And their present.

When they arrived at the Henshaw's spread, Marcus was nowhere in sight and his mother informed Libby he was out riding fences with his father. With as many miles of fence as the Henshaws owned, it was an all day job and then some to check for any repairs that needed to be done along their fence rows. Mrs. Henshaw told her where to put the mule. Dobbie hobbled along behind her and smiled when she said a sad goodbye to the mule.

He put his arm around her and leaned on her as they made their way back to the house, using her for support. They stayed to visit with Mrs. Henshaw for a while before heading home, and she promised to make sure Marcus knew the pie was from Libby.

"Too bad your boyfriend Mr. Kissyface wasn't there," Dobbie said when they were back in the truck. She figured his leg must be hurting to make him so petulant. She had come prepared and handed him pain reliever and some water before they took off.

"Thank you," he said appreciatively and downed the pills. "How did you know?"

"Who knows you better than me?" she asked.

"No one," he said sincerely and reached across the seat to take her hand. "I think Mrs. Henshaw was disappointed to see me today."

"Why? She likes you." Everyone in their community liked Dobbie. He had always been a fun-loving guy and a hard worker. Before their deaths, his parents had been equally well regarded.

"She has big plans for you and her son, and she thinks I'm in the way." He paused, waiting for her to admit or deny it.

"I'm not used to you being jealous over me," she said.

"I'm not jealous," he argued.

She cocked an eyebrow at him.

"Maybe a little," he admitted.

She raised the other eyebrow.

"Okay, a whole lot. I'd like to drop him off in the middle of nowhere and leave him for dead, but it would probably still be his land anyway." He grimaced, picked up his leg, and moved it. "When I think of him kissing you for an entire year, I could…I can't even think of an adjective bad enough."

"I think it's cute." She reached across the seat and poked him. He wrenched away and winced when he jostled his sore leg.

"I bet you wouldn't think it was so cute if the shoe was on the other foot."

"Wrong. A lady is a lady always. I can't picture myself ever behaving badly over some other girl."

"It's a moot point, I guess. All the many, many, *many* girls I met are far away." He glanced at her to gauge her reaction, and she schooled her features into a placid smile. Deflated, he turned to stare out his window with a grimace. At the moment he wasn't certain which bothered him more, his leg that had been clamped in a bear trap or the thought of Libby with Marcus Henshaw.

For the next two days Libby found menial jobs around the house and made them seem like emergencies that required Dobbie's immediate attention. He saw through her, but allowed her to keep him home because he knew she was worried about him. And if he was being honest, he enjoyed the babying she heaped on him. No one besides Libby ever fussed over him. Maggie was outside all day like usual, Kitty was spending a couple of days at her friend Cecily's house, and they were alone, but Libby still refused to kiss Dobbie whenever he tried. And as the days went on and he began feeling better, he tried often, but Libby always rebuffed him.

"Libby, come *on*," he said on Friday when she brought him breakfast. He grabbed her hand and tried to pull her closer. "We're alone. Do you know how miraculous that is?"

She did, but she also realized how dangerous it was. With Dobbie, there could be no in between. She would either have to be all in or all out. Neither of them was ready for all in, so to Libby's way of thinking it was better not to get started at all. She tugged her hand out of his grasp and replaced it with a muffin. "Eat your food and be good, cowboy."

He scowled at her, but hunger won out and he ate the muffin in sullen silence.

By Saturday he couldn't take it any more. "Don't you have any emotions?" he exclaimed after she had rebuffed his advances yet again. "From where I sit, you're a stone cold ice princess."

He stormed out of the house as best he could on his still-injured leg, but came back almost immediately. "I'm sorry." She was standing at the sink with her back to him, and she wouldn't turn around. "Libby, I'm sorry. I blew up and said something stupid, big surprise, but I didn't mean it. Please look at me."

She shook her head. He strode forward, turned her toward him, and realized she was crying soundlessly.

"Ah, Libby," he said, and gently wiped her tears with the edge of his shirt. "I'm sorry."

"I want to, Dobbie, don't you know how much I want to let go? But I'm trying to be wise, for both of us, and not start something that would only be doomed. We're too different, and you know it."

He didn't know it anymore, and he wasn't sure how to convince her. But it broke his heart to see her cry, so he simply gathered her to him and held her so tightly it almost hurt.

"Please stop crying, Libby, please. You're killing me."

She did stop crying then, but that was worse because with no tears as a buffer there was only the unbearable attraction simmering between them. Neither of them was able to let go of the other. She placed a light kiss on his neck and saw the muscles cord there as he fought for control.

"Libby," he said warningly.

"I don't care anymore. I don't care about the consequences." She pulled away so she was whisper close to his lips. "I want…"

The doorbell rang, and they froze at the unexpected sound. They so rarely received visitors; it was a wonder the thing still worked.

"I'll get it," Dobbie said and reluctantly let her go.

She used his absence to check her face in the toaster. Her mascara was smeared and she dabbed at it before applying more gloss.

"Libby," Dobbie said, and the odd inflection in his tone made her turn and look at him in question. Next to him stood a very tall, very pretty girl dressed head to toe in expensive cowgirl paraphernalia that molded to every curve of her shapely figure. "This is Callista," he continued. "We met in Wyoming last year. She's on break from the rodeo. Is it all right if she stays here for a couple of days?"

Right away Libby noticed two things. The first was the way Dobbie was now smiling at her as if at any moment he expected her to fly into a jealous rage and throw Callista out of the house. The second was the possessive way the girl's hand snaked around Dobbie's bicep so Libby was in real danger of flying into said jealous rage.

Instead she summoned her sweetest smile. "Of course she can stay. Why would you have to ask? It's your home, too." She extended her hand to Callista. "Welcome to Montana. I've never been to Wyoming, but I've heard it's lovely. I hope you'll get a chance to rest while you're here. May I help you with your bags? Unfortunately Dobbie has sustained an injury."

Before Callista could speak Dobbie jumped in.

"I am perfectly capable of carrying bags, Elizabeth. I've allowed you to coddle me for an entire week, but I'm done."

He was so oblivious, Libby thought, so hopelessly clueless. Callista had been looking at her with a friendly smile, but Dobbie's tirade tipped her off that Libby was a rival. Her expression changed immediately to patronizing.

"Aren't you the sweetest little thing?" Callista said. "Dobbie told me all about the ranch and the three girls who are like his little sisters. I can't wait to see every bit of it."

Previously Libby had been like his little sister, so that remark didn't bother her. What hurt was that Dobbie had apparently shared intimate family information with this stranger, which indicated more of a relationship than a flirtation.

"Yes, we're all fond of our brother Dobbie," she said in a sickly sweet little girl sort of way. "Why don't you hobble out to the car and get your friend's bags so I can show her to her room, big brother? I'm sure she would like to settle in." She made a shooing motion she knew would infuriate his pride.

He gave her a thunderous look but turned to do her bidding, and Callista followed him.

She heard him enter with the bags and walked into the living room in time to prevent a kiss. Callista gave her a scathing look as if she had planned it on purpose, but Dobbie almost looked relieved. She turned away to hide her smile. He might want her to be jealous, but he didn't want Callista, of that much she was certain. Somehow the knowledge made the situation bearable.

"We'll put you in Anne's room," Libby said. "Dobbie has been using it, but I guess he's ready to go back to the bunkhouse. I changed the sheets this morning so you're all set." She opened the door to Anne's room and turned to see Callista inside. Callista wasn't paying attention to her, though; she was looking at Dobbie in sympathetic understanding.

"You've been sleeping in Anne's room? Oh, my poor Dobbie. That must have been painful for you."

Libby studied Dobbie. Had it been painful? She had wondered if it would be, but he didn't seem bothered by it. Rather he seemed uncomfortable with Callista's display. "Would you like to go riding?" he asked.

"You already know the answer to that," Callista said, and this time she did plaster herself to him for a sloppy kiss.

Don't mind me, Libby wanted to say. *And, no, I don't want to go riding with you. I'll stay here and slave over your supper.* Instead she smiled as if she was enjoying watching their love play. "Have a nice time, you two."

"Oh, we will, Lucy," Callista said

"It's Libby," Dobbie corrected.

She knows, Libby wanted to say. Instead she kept her serene smile until she felt like her face might crack. She saw them to the door and then threw a pillow at it after it closed. At first she scuttled her supper plans and searched her mind for an impressive menu, but stopped short on her way to the kitchen.

"No," she said out loud. "This is who I am, and if it's not good enough for Shane Dobbins and his rodeo Amazon, then so be it." With that cheerful thought in mind, she returned to the kitchen and resumed working on supper.

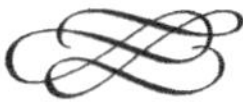

CHAPTER 17

Callista and Dobbie rode for hours. When they sat at the supper table that night, Libby knew by his grimace his leg was killing him. She quietly set two pain reliever tablets beside his plate, and gently patted his shoulder. He flashed her a grateful smile and Callista's eyes narrowed ominously.

"Did you make this, Luby?" she asked, pointing to the stew.

"I did," Libby replied.

"That's the best part of travel," Callista continued. "You get to taste regional dishes and simple country fare."

"You can taste it every day of the week here," Libby said flippantly. She sat to dish up her own "simple country fare." Her spirits lifted when Kitty gave her an amused glance. Kitty was an observer, and she had a wicked sense of humor. Libby crossed her eyes at her as if to indicate she was simple, and Kitty hid her giggle in her bite of bread.

Maggie launched into an excited narrative about Callista. Apparently she had spent the afternoon performing tricks from the rodeo, and Maggie was enthralled.

"You don't ride bulls?" Libby asked. Bull riding was her only experience with the rodeo.

"No, I'm a trick pony rider. Of course I couldn't do everything today on horses who haven't been trained with me," Callista said.

"You mean there's more?" Maggie asked in awe. They could all see the wheels turning in her head.

"Maggie, don't try anything you saw her do," her father warned, and Libby breathed a sigh of relief. Maggie wasn't a daredevil like Anne, but she had an affinity for animals, and she would probably be convinced she could never get hurt on a horse.

"But Dad," Maggie started, but he cut her off with a look.

"It's bad enough you ride your pony bareback. Don't give me more to worry about," he said.

She let out a sigh, but everyone knew she would obey. Of all the sisters Maggie was the sweetest and most docile.

After supper everyone gathered in the living room except Maggie and their father who went riding. Libby pulled out her needles and started to knit one of the sweaters she had received an order for.

"Oh, and you knit, too," Callista said. "You're like my grandma. She wears the same style dress." She turned her attention back to Dobbie, and the two of them talked about mutual acquaintances in Wyoming.

Libby listened with a disapproving ear. It sounded like Dobbie had gone a bit wild during his time away from home, and her suspicions were confirmed when he started to shoot her furtive glances and change the subject.

Callista was having none of that, though, and detailed the places they had visited together, places like bars where they had apparently stayed all night on more than one occasion.

Libby had to work to keep her expression impassive.

It was none of her business, she repeated to herself over and over. He wasn't hers. Somehow that thought hurt more than the hearing about Dobbie's brief period of rebellion.

A little while later Dobbie said a pointed goodnight and let himself out. Callista followed him and came back a minute later looking angry. Libby waited until the other girl went upstairs before she put aside her knitting and started to turn out the lights. It was later than she usually went to bed. Everyone else was already gone, but there was no way she would have left Dobbie and Callista alone on the couch. With Callista's predatory instincts, it would be like leaving a baby gazelle with a panther.

She turned off the last light. A hand grasped her upper arm, and another hand covered her mouth.

"Don't scream, it's me," Dobbie said.

Libby shoved his hand away from her face. "Of course it's you. Who else would it be?"

He chuckled. "Does anything ruffle you, Libby? Anything besides grizzlies and the possibility of failure, I mean."

"No. Those are my only two fears. Goodnight." She tried to step around him, but he rested his hands on her waist and held her fast.

"We have some unfinished business between us," he said warmly.

"You have got to be kidding," she said, and her tone held no answering warmth.

"I am, but it was worth a try. I need to talk to you about what she said tonight."

"It's none of my business," she said.

"It's all of your business, and I need you to know. I went a little wild when I left home, but not as bad as she made it sound. I was mostly an observer, peering into a life we've never known to see how the other half lives. Turns out it wasn't for me. I actually *am* a simple country boy."

"I'm glad," she said sincerely. "Although you know my feelings would be the same if you had rebelled when you went away. I know who you are in here." She tapped his chest.

He pulled her closer, urging her head against his chest. She readily complied, pressing her ear to his heart, enjoying its steady rhythm. She had grown used to the sound over all the long hours they'd spent on the trail, Libby cradled in his embrace. He kissed the top of her head and rubbed her back in a slow, soothing circle. He was so gentle with her. Previously she would never have guessed he was so tender.

"Want to know a secret?" he whispered.

She smiled in anticipation. "What?"

"You're my girl, Libby Chapman." He gave her a squeeze, kissed the top of her head once more, and let her go. "Now go upstairs so I can lock up."

She took a step back, kissed her finger, touched it to his cheek, and went inside.

The next day was church. Callista tried to get Dobbie to stay home with her, but he was adamant.

"This family goes to church on Sundays," he said. It seemed to Libby he was getting more hostile to Callista as the minutes ticked, so she redoubled her efforts to be nice to the girl. It chafed her sense of hospitality to see a houseguest mistreated, but Callista didn't make it easy. She sensed Dobbie pulling away from her, and she increased her efforts to insult Libby. She picked and sniped at Libby on the long drive to church and all through lunch.

Libby kept her smile in place and didn't say a word, but it was getting harder to do. She wanted to defend herself, but she didn't want to appear jealous.

After lunch she took up her knitting again, and again Callista commented on her grandmotherliness. She had reached her limit by that point, so she stood to go, but Dobbie stood, too. He placed Libby protectively behind him and turned to Callista.

"That's it. You have to go. Libby is too sweet and ladylike to say anything, but I'm not. Your treatment of her is uncalled for, to say the least. She has been nothing but kind to you, and you have trampled her hospitality. I'll help you with your bags, and then I never want to see or hear from you again."

Callista stood and stormed from the room.

"I'll help her with her bags," an amused Kitty said. She had been so quiet Libby didn't know she was in the room until she spoke. She stood and followed Callista. Dobbie and Libby stood frozen in place until they heard the front door close.

"Thank you," Libby said.

Dobbie whirled toward her, livid. "What does it take to make you jealous, woman?"

"Why would I need to be jealous of a stranger when I have my sister's memory hovering between us?"

His jaw fell. He never realized his relationship with Anne might bother her, but of course it did. She couldn't see inside his head to know how different things were with her. "Libby, it wasn't like that with Anne."

Her wounded eyes told him she didn't believe him. "I know you went shopping for an engagement ring the summer before you both left."

"Yes, but," he started, but she held up a hand to stop him.

"It's fine, Dobbie. Meeting Callista reminded me of something I had almost forgotten. We're not right for each other. Girls like Anne and Callista, girls who can spend ten hours in the saddle and rope a steer, those are the girls for you."

"And who is the man for you? Some cultured city slicker who can't open a jar of pickles?"

"I don't know, and right now I don't care. I'm too confused to want anything with anyone." Tears pooled in her eyes, but she refused to let them brim over.

"Libby," he said in a pained tone. It killed him to see her hurting, especially when he knew it was his fault. He reached for her, but she took a step back.

"I can't, I just can't. You have to stop this. Please." She turned and fled to the barn where she sat in the soft hay, buried her face in the fur of a newborn kitten, and finally allowed her tears to fall.

CHAPTER 18

For the next few days Libby and Dobbie cautiously avoided each other. She thought he was giving her space, but she didn't see the calculating look in his eyes as he studied her over the supper table.

"Go to the fair with me tomorrow," he said, and she dropped a cucumber before whirling to face him. It was the middle of the day, and she thought he was out riding fences.

"I can't go to the fair, I'm too busy," she said. Her garden harvest was in full swing, and she was preserving food like a woman possessed.

"I'm the foreman of this ranch, and all areas of ranch life fall under my jurisdiction, including kitchen help. Technically that makes you my employee, so if I say you have to take a vacation day tomorrow, then you have to take a vacation day tomorrow. Don't make me fire you, Miss Chapman."

She gave him a wry smile. "Try and replace me, Mr. Dobbins."

"Can't. You're irreplaceable. Come on, your little sister is showing her chickens and her turkey this week. You have to be a supportive big sister."

"My sister shows her chickens and turkeys every year," she pointed out.

"And when is the last time you made it to the fair?" he countered.

He had her there. Every year she added more work and became busier. She honestly couldn't remember the last time she made it to the fair, and suddenly she really wanted to go.

"All right, Dobbie," she agreed shyly.

"Great," he said, looking like a little boy on Christmas morning. "We'll get an early start tomorrow. Maggie is going with us. Do you think Kitty will go?"

"Only if she thinks they'll have a library exhibit," she said distractedly, her attention once more on the pickles she was preparing.

Dobbie had his own work, but he remained in the doorway, unwilling to leave her when she looked so fresh and pretty and happy. Her cheeks were flushed the way they were whenever she was working, which happened to be all the time. The kitchen had rapidly become his favorite place on the ranch since his return, mostly because Libby was there filling it with her presence. He could stay all day doing nothing but stare at her as she bustled from counter to fridge to stove and back again. Alas his work won out, and he turned to go with a reluctant sigh.

The fair was over an hour away on the other side of their small town. Their county was large and spread out to accommodate so many sprawling ranches. The fair was the social event of the season. Friends and neighbors who rarely saw each other gathered to show off their produce and livestock and exchange information and gossip. It was especially fun for kids who not only got to ride rides but spent time with their friends while they showed their animals. Competition was fierce where people's livelihoods depended on the animals they showed, and each family strove to put their best foot forward for fair week. When Dobbie was a boy, he and Anne showed cows, but that was where the beef stopped. Libby had occasionally entered food, but she had never gotten into livestock. Neither had Kitty, who occasionally entered some of her photography. Maggie was the last of the family and the most interested in animals, but she didn't have the heart to show cows because it required a competitive killer instinct she lacked. She stuck with chickens and turkeys.

Maggie sat in the truck between Libby and Dobbie and chatted happily the whole way about the week's events. Libby and Dobbie watched her with equally affectionate smiles, occasionally making eye contact over her head. Maggie was the darling of the family, and for good reason. She had always been a little ray of sunshine—cheerful, sweet, and innocent. She was easygoing and unspoiled and almost never cross or out of sorts. Thoughtful, tender-hearted, and always ready to help, everyone agreed Maggie was special.

They arrived at the fair. Maggie immediately wanted to run and find her friends, but Libby was reluctant to let her go.

"Lib, she's fourteen," Dobbie reminded her. "She's old enough to spend the day on her own, and she knows how to find us if she needs us."

Libby turned back to Maggie, who was pleading for release with her big, soft eyes. "Be careful, and be good, and don't talk to strangers, and don't follow anyone anywhere, even if they say they need help," she admonished.

Maggie nodded, hugged her tightly, and ran off.

Libby watched her go. "I worry about her."

Dobbie smiled and squeezed her shoulders bracingly. "She'll be fine. She's smart, despite her trusting nature. Besides, I have spies everywhere, and they're keeping an eye on her for me."

That was probably true. Maggie was something of a pet of everyone in the community. No doubt everyone would be watching out for her today, but Libby had been mothering her for eight years, and old habits died hard.

They started in the produce building. "Your stuff looks better than this, Lib. Why don't you ever enter anything anymore?"

"I've become too practical in my old age. I would rather sell it than display it, I guess."

"But if you won here then you could add 'Award Winning' to your labels," he said.

"I never thought of that," she mused.

"You and I aren't so different in our desires. I have big plans for the ranch." His easygoing smile fled and slid into a frown.

"What? What is it?" Libby asked, ever sensitive to his pain or discomfort.

"It's nothing," he said with a shake of his head.

"Come on, Dobbie, tell me. Please."

"I was thinking about the ranch, about my plans for it. Marrying Anne was a way to make the ranch a permanent home, I guess, and I still haven't come to terms with the fact that the dream is over."

"Dobbie," Libby exclaimed. "What are you talking about? You're our family. The ranch is your permanent home. It's as much yours as it is mine or any of my sisters. You're like a son to Dad."

"The key word is 'like.' I'm not his son, Libby, and blood is always thicker than water. What happens when you marry, or Kitty, or Maggie? Your husbands will have first claim to the land, as they should. They're not going to want an outsider sticking around telling them how to run it."

That Dobbie would feel this way upset her more than she would have thought possible. She hurt for him, and the pain went deep. Not only had he lost Anne, but he had lost his future and his home. "You are not an outsider, don't ever say that again. You're ours, and we're yours, forever. Besides, I'm next in line after Anne, and if she doesn't want it the ranch goes to me. You will always have a home here, Dobbie. Always."

"You say that now, and it's sweet, but it's not practical. You're going away. Who knows where you'll end up, or with whom?"

She wanted to argue, but he was right. How could she guarantee him a future when she didn't know what hers held? Instead she shoved aside their deep and depressing thoughts and gave him a poke. "You said 'whom.'"

He slung his arm around her shoulders and bussed her cheek, as ready to lighten the mood as she was. "Even cowboys use proper grammar some of the time, Elizabeth."

She smiled and tugged his sleeve to lead him to the livestock barn.

"Do you miss your old glory days at the fair?" she asked. He and

Anne and Marcus Henshaw always had a running competition to see who would walk away with the beef award every year. It was always one of the three of them, but when Anne or Dobbie won it was celebrated equally. Anything to beat the Henshaws.

"Sometimes I do," he said. "Life was simpler then."

She smiled, but it didn't reach her eyes. He must miss Anne so much. They had a lot of years, a lot of experiences, and a lot of common interests between them. Was she a pale substitute for her sister? She thought so, and the thought was bruising.

"But simple isn't always better," he continued. "I know who I am now, and I know what I want. The only thing I don't know is how to get it." He gave her a pointed glance from the corner of his eye, one she was too lost in thought to notice.

"I used to be envious of Anne because she always made the fair sound like so much fun," Libby said, remembering the days long ago when Anne and Dobbie went to the fair and seemingly took all the fun with them.

"You would have hated it. We were hot and filthy all week long, and the boredom got so bad at times that we had to be creative to keep ourselves entertained," he said.

The kids who showed livestock spent the week at the fair sleeping near their animals. Libby wasn't sure if it was necessity or tradition that mandated the practice, but the kids looked forward to it every year. Maggie had begged to be allowed to stay all week, but Libby wouldn't hear of it. Thankfully neither would her father or Dobbie, so she settled for spending her days at the fair and coming home every night.

"Anne and I used to think up pranks to pull on Marcus. He was only two years older, but when we were young he seemed grown up and mature, so we tried to bring him down a few pegs. Anne thought up some doozies, as you can imagine."

He wore a nostalgic smile, and Libby turned her face away. There was no way she could compete with her spirited and outrageous sister. Anne was an irrepressible fireball, and Libby was a baby mouse in comparison. What good were pies and embroidered handkerchiefs next to exciting stunts and pranks? Callista was right. Libby was exactly like someone's grandmother. What other seventeen year old spent her days canning, pickling, knitting, and tending the garden? None she knew.

"You miss her," Libby said sympathetically.

"I miss her friendship," Dobbie said. He started to elaborate further, but Libby pulled him over to the poultry barn, and they got caught up looking for Maggie and her chickens.

Dobbie bought her a corndog for lunch, and they shared an iced tea. After they ate they watched a hog-calling contest. Dobbie put his arm around her in the darkened building, and she snuggled up close to him and closed her eyes. For this moment she wanted to pretend they were really together, that he was hers, that he had never been Anne's, and that she wasn't going away in a few short weeks. All too soon the event was over, and they resumed their tour of the fair.

"Libby," a girl's voice called, and Libby turned to look.

"Heather," she exclaimed and stepped forward to hug her old friend. Friends were few and far between, even more so as she grew up. When they were little, her mother had insisted they make the long drive into town to attend school with other children, but after her death, the four girls withdrew from public school and switched to home-schooling instead. It was practical because it saved a two hour commute each day, but it was lonely, too. Their father rationalized that since there were four of them, plus Dobbie, they wouldn't mind the isolation. But they did, and slowly their friends had frittered away for everyone except Kitty. Her friend Cecily lived on a neighboring ranch, and the two girls were close.

"I would have recognized you anywhere," Heather said. "You're the only one here today in a dress."

Wearing a dress every day had become so much a part of her she didn't think about it until people pointed it out. And it was so much a part of her she didn't feel slighted, if that had been Heather's intent.

"Hello, Dobbie." Heather turned interested eyes to him. "I haven't seen you in ages."

"I went away for a couple of years," he said.

"I'm glad you came back," Heather said flirtatiously.

"Me, too," Dobbie said. He eased his arm around Libby's waist, and Heather raised her eyebrows in surprise.

"Oh," she drawled, her eyes sliding questioningly toward Libby.

Libby's eyes gave nothing away, but she did inch closer to Dobbie and rest her hand possessively on his stomach. Heather was a pretty and vivacious girl. It was better to curtail any intentions she had toward Dobbie before they got started.

"Are you still going to college in the fall?" Libby asked her.

"Yes, are you?" Her question was weighted with equal parts curiosity and cunning. Libby had the mental image of her waiting at the end of the driveway until Libby's car pulled away and then pouncing on a newly available Dobbie.

"I think so," Libby said slowly. Beside her Dobbie tensed, and she didn't know if it was from hurt or curiosity over the hesitation in her tone.

They made small talk with Heather for a few more minutes and said goodbye, going their separate ways.

"Well that's that," Libby said.

"What?"

"Heather's a gossip and a half. By the end of the day, everyone will know about us."

"And what will they know?" he asked.

"That…That we…They'll think we…Oh, you know," she said, and looked away in embarrassment.

He chuckled and took her hand, linking their fingers together for all the world to see, namely their neighbors and friends. She glanced at him in sharp surprise, and he smiled. "In for a penny, in for a pound," he said.

She smiled and squeezed his hand. "I suppose so."

CHAPTER 19

*E*ach night the fair held a special event. Libby hadn't kept up on the fair for years, so she had no idea what event was planned for this night.

"I hope it's the demolition derby," she said, and Dobbie laughed.

"I never would have guessed my little Libby was so bloodthirsty."

"Sometimes a lady likes to see things get smashed to bits," she replied, grinding her fist into her palm.

They ate supper at the agricultural building. Several local charity groups came together and cooked for the week and split the profits for their organization. The food was good, and the portions were large. They lingered over supper as they talked about the food, the weather, the people around them, and the things they had seen that day. For Libby, it was a rare reprieve from cooking.

"I hope Maggie's eating well," she said.

"She probably has boys vying for the chance to buy supper for her," Dobbie said. "Not that she'll notice."

Maggie was a late bloomer in her interests, but not in looks. The thought of dating boys hadn't yet occurred to her, but outwardly she was beautiful with long almost blond hair and luminous brown eyes. Boys adored her, as did everyone who met her, but she paid them no notice, assigning everyone buddy status. Perversely, they liked her all the more for it. There was usually a crowd of boys vying for her attention, but she was oblivious to their interest and treated them all with equal good cheer.

"I think Marcus's little brother, Mathew, is especially sweet on her," Libby said. "He used to tag along an awful lot whenever Marcus came to visit, and the two of them have been close playmates since they were in diapers."

Dobbie clenched his napkin in his fist. He and Marcus had never been close friends, but lately thoughts of the other man made him murderously angry. "I hope Maggie is too smart to go for looks and money."

"What else is there?" Libby asked.

Dobbie sat up straighter and prepared for a lecture when he realized she was teasing him. "There's chemistry, and attraction, and fun, and friendship, and a lifetime of memories and mutual understanding," he said instead, leaning over the table to kiss her on the forehead.

"People are staring at us," she told him, her cheeks blushing a flattering shade of pink.

"Then let's give them a good show."

She leaned closer and closed the distance between them. "No."

"Then let's go somewhere private," he said.

"There's nowhere private here. There are people everywhere, and we know all of them," she said.

"You're forgetting how much time I spent here as a kid. I know *lots* of private places." He reached for her hands, cradling them between them.

He was right, she had forgotten. Unfortunately with the reminder came the knowledge he had likely found those places with Anne. She wouldn't allow him to lead her to a private nook where he had also kissed her sister. She snatched her hands from his grasp, cleared their plates, and stormed out the door without waiting to see if he followed.

Of course he did follow, and he had no idea why she was suddenly so angry with him. It seemed like he couldn't get anything right near her anymore, and the thought frustrated him.

"Libby," he began.

"I don't want to talk about it," she said.

They walked in awkward, heavy silence until seven o'clock, and then he took her hand and tugged her toward the main arena.

It was a good sign she didn't withdraw her hand from his grasp, and her anger dissolved completely when they arrived at the stadium.

"Oh, the dance," she gasped, and he smiled at the excitement in her voice. Every year the fair held a massive dance with a live band as one of the nightly events. "I didn't know it was tonight. Did you?"

"Maybe," he said. In truth he had planned this night especially to bring her. He wanted to dance with her and forget everything else. "I did a lot of dancing in Texas. Do you think you can keep up?"

"We won't know until I try," she said. She loved dancing, but she was rusty.

But before they could reach the dance floor, they were waylaid by a young cowboy who caught Dobbie's attention.

"I thought you left for parts unknown, Dobbie," he said.

The two men shook hands as Dobbie replied. "I did. What are you doing at our fair? I thought you Kings stayed in your own county."

Libby's eyes widened in surprise. The Kings owned a huge ranch in Culliver county. It was almost as vast as the Henshaw's spread. The four King brothers were practically legendary for their good looks. She had never seen them in person, and she could barely see this one now with Dobbie actively trying to block her view.

"I came to look at the cattle and see what you all have going on over here. Plus, I like to have fun." He leaned around Dobbie to grin at Libby and she suddenly understood what all the fuss was about. He was ridiculously attractive, with sandy brown hair and pretty eyes that practically sparkled with mischief. One cheek sported a dimple so deep she was oddly tempted to poke it to see how far in her finger would go. At last when it became obvious Dobbie wasn't going to introduce them, he stuck out his hand.

"I'm Coy King," he said, his tone somehow both polite and flirtatious.

Libby placed her hand in his. "Libby Chapman."

Now it was his turn to look surprised. He kept her hand and glanced at Dobbie. "Aren't you foreman for the Chapmans?"

"Yes, I am," Dobbie said. Libby looked at Dobbie, trying to understand why his tone was suddenly studded with ice when a moment ago he and Coy had been talking like old friends.

Coy's smile increased so his dimple became cavernous. "Would you care to take a turn on the dance floor with me, Libby?" She couldn't be sure, but she thought he might have fluttered his long eyelashes at her.

"No, she wouldn't," Dobbie said. He grasped their hands and pulled them apart. "Go find a girl in your own county, King."

Libby was mortified, but Coy laughed. "Ah, it's like that, is it?"

"It's like that," Dobbie said. He pulled Libby onto the dance floor, away from the other man.

"Nice to meet you," she called as Dobbie practically dragged her away from Coy. She tossed him an apologetic smile. He gave her a two-fingered little salute, looking highly amused.

"Dobbie, you were rude to him," she said accusingly. Dobbie was usually congenial and unfailingly polite, especially to a near stranger he rarely saw.

"Coy understands," he assured her.

"I don't," she said. She wasn't at all sure she liked this brutish, possessive side of him.

"Libby, Coy has a certain reputation. When I saw him eyeing you… let's say sometimes a man has to stake a claim, and that can't be done with soft words and smiles."

Her nose wrinkled. "You make me sound like a mountain you discovered."

"You gave me a great idea. Would you consider wearing a flag with my name on it?"

"What do you think?" she asked.

He tightened his arms around her and leaned down to rest his forehead on hers. "I think I'm going to have to do *something* to keep other men away."

"What other men? Coy is the only other man who has approached me today."

"Maybe. But they're looking at you like they want to pluck you out of my arms, plop you in their saddle, and ride off into the sunset with you."

"Dobbie, for as long as you've known me you've been telling me men are interested in me."

"And I've always been correct."

"You're crazy. Boys don't notice me; they never have."

"Libby, trust me on this one issue, okay? You have no idea the way guys look at you, but I do. From the time you started to became a teenager, men have been mesmerized with you. You're beautiful and feminine, a good cook, smart, funny, and a little bit of a spitfire. If you have flaws, I have no idea what they are."

He was well aware of her flaws, but she was flattered, nonetheless. "What about you? You're a charmer, and you're handsome. Girls love you."

"Do they?" he asked innocently. "Do they really?" He was trying to get her to confess her feelings for him, but she refused to be sucked in. They swayed gently to the music for a little while, looking into each other's eyes. Eventually it dawned on them the music was a raucous square dance and they were the only couple still slow dancing.

They moved off the dance floor and stood to the side with the other spectators. Dobbie kept his arm possessively around her as they watched the square dance. His thumb slid gently along her waist, and Libby felt herself melting, melting. More than a few curious glances dodged their way. By the end of the evening it would be all over town that she and Dobbie were a couple, but she was having a difficult time feeling upset over the potential gossip. Let them talk. She and Dobbie knew the truth. They knew they were…What exactly were they?

The song switched and he looked down at her. "I learned a few things when I was down south. Want to give it a try?"

"Yes, please," she said, and followed him back onto the dance floor.

He started a Texas two step, and went slowly while she learned.

"I'm glad you're wearing a dress," he said. "I like to dance with a girl in a dress. It's weird to dance with someone else who's wearing pants."

"I wouldn't know. I've never danced with anyone who was wearing a dress."

"Good to know," he said. He gave her a light spin, and her cheeks flushed with pleasure as her dress flared around her knees.

"You're a good dancer, Dobbie."

"One of my many talents."

"And so modest," she said, and he laughed.

They danced together until the fair closed down. A few of the dances were line dances. They participated in those and had fun, but otherwise they stayed glued together, gently swaying to the music.

"This is nice," Libby said. She was only partly referring to the dance. The night felt like a reprieve from their regular lives. She wasn't sure what the morning would bring between them, but for this one night he was hers, and the feeling was better than she could have imagined.

"It doesn't have to end, Libby."

She didn't reply. She didn't want to talk about their hopeless situation, and she certainly didn't want to argue. It was better to ignore the topic and live for the moment.

The dance finished and they walked hand in hand to the truck.

Dobbie opened the door and lifted Libby inside. He didn't have to, of course. She was perfectly capable of climbing into the tall cab by herself, but he wanted, no *needed* to touch her. He rested his hands on her hips, and they stared at each other, the tension between them suddenly at full boil. Libby put her hands on his face and leaned in to whisper.

"Come inside the truck, Shane."

He closed her door, bounded to his side, and vaulted inside. The slam of his door felt unnaturally loud next to the sudden stillness of the cab. She was breathing hard. Or maybe it was him. Maybe it was both of them.

"Do you think they can see us?" Libby asked as she stared out at the herds of people swarming by the truck.

"At this point do you care?" He turned to look at her. She was so beautiful with the dim moonlight glinting off her perfect face.

"No." She turned to face him, and it felt like the moment before a bomb goes off.

Fingers shaking, his free hand reached up and touched her cheek. "Lib." He let go her hand and grasped her waist, but before he could pull her to him the passenger door opened.

"I almost forgot where we were parked," Maggie's cheerful voice announced. She started to climb over Libby to sit in the middle, her usual spot, but Libby held her back. She slid to the middle, forcing Maggie to settle next to the door. Maggie gave her a puzzled look but didn't comment. The youngest always had to sit in the middle because the gearshift was there, and it was uncomfortable. It had always been that way in their family, one of the unspoken rules of seniority.

"You look tired, sweetie," Libby said by way of explanation. "Try to go to sleep."

Maggie nodded and rested her head in Libby's lap. Almost as soon as they left the parking lot she was asleep.

Libby smiled up at Dobbie and rested her hand on his thigh. She had to press close to him to avoid the gearshift. After a few minutes he put his arm around her, and she laid her head on his shoulder.

"Dobbie," she whispered.

"What?" he whispered, too.

"The middle's not so bad."

He kissed the top of her head, and they made the rest of the trip in silence.

CHAPTER 20

For the next three days until her birthday, Dobbie didn't seek Libby out. At supper he studied her with a speculative expression, but he didn't speak to her directly. That was why, on the fourth day, it came as a surprise to her he still wanted to take her out.

He wouldn't say where they were going, but he did tell her to wear something nice. So she traded in her usual calf-length flared dresses for her little black dress. She had bought it to go on fancy dates with Marcus, not an ideal thought to reuse it for Dobbie. But Libby was too practical to buy a new dress for each man in her life.

The dress had spaghetti straps and stopped slightly above her knees. She stood looking in the mirror, considering her hair. A French twist had become her daily standard. Not only did it keep hair off her face when she was cooking, but it helped the elegant image she tried to maintain. Tonight she decided to leave it down. It curled in soft waves after so many hours spent in a twist, and she realized she liked it that way. Maybe she would wear it that way more often. The thought gave her a giddy sense of freedom, and she smiled at her reflection as she applied more makeup than her usual gloss and mascara. At last she stood back to appraise her appearance and was taken aback by what she saw. The girl in the mirror looked older and sophisticated, like the sort of girl who routinely went on dates with handsome men. Not at all like the kind of girl who, up until two hours ago, had been pickling cucumbers.

She was almost as surprised by Dobbie's appearance as he was by hers. He always wore his Stetson, and when he didn't he had a ring around his head from where it had been, but not tonight. His thick sandy blond hair was perfectly and stylishly arrayed, and he wore a spotless suit she didn't know he owned. It fit him like a glove and it was immaculate, like the rest of him. He held out his clean hands for her inspection.

"Impressive," she said, and she didn't merely mean his clean hands.

Dobbie clasped her hands and pulled her close, but it was the middle of the day, and there were too many prying eyes. Since Callista's visit, everyone had been alerted to the simmering tension between Libby and Dobbie, and they felt they were being watched all the time now. There was no one more gossipy than an old cowboy, her grandmother used to say.

"You look incredible," Dobbie whispered. "The most beautiful I've ever seen you, and that's saying something because you're beautiful every day, Libby."

She pressed her palms to his freshly shaved cheeks. "And you look incredibly handsome. You clean up well, Mr. Dobbins."

"Only for you, Miss Chapman. Ready?"

"Ready," she agreed, and he led her to the truck.

Once again, she sat pressed to his side in the middle seat. He parked at the depot, and Libby's insides lit with a spark of excitement. She had thought they were going to the diner in town. Now it appeared as if he had something grander in mind.

"We're taking the train?"

"We're taking the train," he answered, but wouldn't tell her more. Their small talk in the car had been pleasant, but they were prevented from further conversation when they boarded the train. The only available seats were near two tourists, who were ecstatic to meet a real cowboy. They spent the hour train ride peppering Dobbie with questions about ranch life. He remained patient and polite, and Libby appreciated his kindness. Her experience with men was limited, but instinct told her not everyone was as caring and considerate. In Libby's mind, those traits went a long way toward displaying good character. If she found it important to always be a lady, she found it equally important that a man always be a gentleman.

He led her to a restaurant in Billings. She had never tried it before, but she didn't get to Billings very often.

"I read about this place in the paper," he said. "It got good reviews, and it seemed like something you would like."

And she did. The owners were chefs who had once worked in New York City. The food was upscale and innovative, and Libby marveled over every dish she and Dobbie tried.

She thought supper was the highlight of the evening, so she almost fell over when he led her to the theater and bought tickets to a Broadway play now touring the country. Libby had seen ads for it, but she never had any hope of seeing it in person. She couldn't believe Dobbie was the one making her unspoken dream come true.

"Who are you?" she whispered before the curtain rose.

"Yours, if you'll have me," he whispered, reaching a hand to caress one of her curls.

Her heart fluttered furiously. He was unexpected. When she thought she had him pegged as the quintessential cowhand, he suddenly flip-flopped and became a sophisticated charmer, wooing her with a fancy dinner and play. She was thankful when the play started and she could shove aside her conflicting thoughts.

The play was amazing, and she told him so over and over. "Did you like it?" she asked tentatively.

"What's not to like? It had good music and an interesting story, like watching a movie live."

His answer delighted her. Impulsively she threw her arms around his neck and leapt, hanging off him so her feet dangled. "Thank you."

Dobbie wrapped his arms around her waist and twirled her around and around in the middle of the deserted sidewalk, until they were both breathless with laughter. The train ground into the station, and they looked at each other in sudden panic. Her father would kill them both if they became stranded in the city overnight.

Dobbie took Libby's hand and practically dragged her to the depot, carrying her the last ten feet. They made it as the doors were starting to close, and Libby clutched at a stitch in her side.

"If you think roping steers is hard work, you should try running in three inch heels," she panted.

"Three inches?" he exclaimed, completely unaffected by the hard sprint. "You always wear heels when we're together. Let me see how tall you are without them."

She took off her shoes and stepped down, feeling suddenly vulnerable as she peered up at him.

"You're a tiny wisp," he said softly. She barely cleared the middle of his chest. "How tall are you?"

"I'm five two," she said.

He gave her a dubious look.

"Almost," she added with a sheepish grin. For a moment they were lost in each other's eyes, and then the train lurched forward as it began to gain speed. The train wasn't as crowded as before, but there were other people in their car. Libby put her shoes back on, and they took their seats. Her gaze was fastened on something outside the window, but when Dobbie took her hand, she turned to look at him.

His head snapped forward, embarrassed at having been caught staring. But now it was Libby's turn to stare, drinking in his handsome profile, the bumpy notch on his crooked nose. He glanced at her, and her eyes darted forward. Smiling, she slowly swiveled toward him again and saw him smiling at her.

"What's wrong with us?" she whispered, but she was still smiling.

"Not a thing," he whispered, grinning like an idiot.

The train was crowded, but they might as well have been alone for all the attention they paid the other passengers. Libby felt mesmerized, giddy, dizzy with emotion, and like she couldn't look away. Dobbie seemed to feel the same. They were saying things with their eyes they couldn't, or wouldn't, say with their words. Dobbie hooked his arm around her neck and kissed her temple. Libby rested her head against him, enjoying the cozy, intimate silence. For this one moment, it felt like the world was at their command and everything would be okay.

When they arrived at their stop it was late, and they still had an hour's drive to get back home.

"Are you okay to drive?" Libby asked when they were settled in the truck. She felt barely awake. She didn't know how he would be able to make the long trek; she certainly couldn't.

"I'm fine," he assured her. "Insomnia, remember? I'm used to being tired."

She ran a soothing hand over his leg. "I hate that you have trouble sleeping."

"Want to know a secret?" he asked.

"Always."

"When we were camping I slept well all week long. I think you have magical powers, Lib." His hand rested on her knee. He brushed his thumb back and forth and she shivered.

"Maybe you were exhausted from all your hard work."

"No. I always work hard. Somehow knowing you were a couple feet away and holding my hand made it all right to sleep." He lightly squeezed her knee. "I need you in all kinds of ways, Libby."

She blushed and was glad he couldn't see. "You made me feel safe that week. I wasn't afraid of the bears or the wolves or the snakes." She shivered again. "How did you ever get me to agree to that?"

"You're a trooper, baby girl."

They sat in easy silence for a while. Libby's eyelids started to droop and she struggled to keep them open.

"Go to sleep, Sweetheart," Dobbie said gently.

"No, I don't want to leave you alone." But even as she said it, she felt herself drifting toward unconsciousness. "Dobbie," she wanted to get it out before she fell asleep. "I loved tonight. My favorite night ever."

"Happy eighteenth birthday, Elizabeth Cahpman," he said, and that was the last thing Libby remembered until morning.

CHAPTER 21

*L*ibby woke the next morning in her pajamas, and was relieved to find out Kitty had been awake when they arrived home. So when Dobbie carried her upstairs, she was the one who changed Libby's clothes.

As a thank you, Libby spent a long time detailing the play for her. If anyone loved culture more than Libby, it was Kitty. It comforted her to think someday she might not be alone in the city because Kitty might want to move there, too. When she asked her about it, Kitty surprised her.

"I don't know. The city is so busy. Here I can read or write or do whatever I want, whenever I want. It's sort of the best of both worlds because I have access to whatever I want and time enough to enjoy it."

Libby thought about that for a long time. Was she wrong in thinking it had to be either one way or the other? Could the ranch somehow offer a compromise that would give her what she wanted? For that matter, what did she want?

That day she felt things change imperceptibly between Dobbie and her, although she couldn't pinpoint how. There was a new sense of belonging between them, even though they still hadn't spoken the words or really ever kissed beyond one gentle kiss in the helicopter.

They stole glances at each other on the sly all through supper. At least they thought they were being sly. In reality everyone was watching them with knowing smiles, even Maggie.

"Kitty and Maggie, why don't you do the dishes tonight and give your sister a break?" their father said. Turning to Dobbie he added, "Maybe you kids can take a walk."

"Sounds good," Dobbie said. He reached across the table, grabbed Libby's hand, and tugged her behind him. She wasn't prepared when he led her to the porch, turned abruptly, and swept her into his arms.

"Remind me to give your dad a nice Christmas present this year," he said, and then his mouth descended toward hers.

She put up a hand to stop him and looked around. "Can people see us?"

"No. I tested this spot from the barn and the house. We're hidden. Why are you stalling?"

"I'm not." She stood on her toes to grant him better access, and then they heard it; an insistent beeping coming from the long lane. They turned to watch the truck approach, but Dobbie didn't let her go. If anything, his arms tightened on her waist.

"You have got to be kidding me," he murmured, but she didn't understand the tension in his voice because she didn't recognize the truck. It wasn't until the passengers descended that she jerked out of Dobbie's arms with a guilty flush and a gasp of surprise.

"Happy belated birthday," Anne called, stopped short, and stared at Dobbie. "You're back."

At the same time, Libby noticed Will step out of the truck behind Anne. She pushed away from Dobbie and ran to Will's welcoming embrace. He picked her up and kissed her cheek before setting her back down. Will was the true big brother of her dreams, and she loved him deeply.

"Hello, Libby," he said. He hugged her tightly once more before turning to look at the porch. "Hello, Dobbie."

"Will," Dobbie said, and gave him a curt nod. He was scowling, but it eased somewhat when Libby moved away from Will.

They were saved from further awkwardness by the appearance of their father.

"What's all the commotion out here?" he asked, and stopped short at the sight of Anne and Will. "You're one for surprises, little girl." He opened his arms and Anne walked into them. He gave her a sedate kiss on the cheek and patted her head. "I almost didn't recognize you, City Slicker."

Libby really looked at Anne for the first time. Her hair was back in a braid, but she wasn't wearing the cowgirl outfit that had been her uniform on the ranch. Instead she wore linen trousers and a sleeveless shirt. She looked grownup and stylish and cool, totally unlike the country girl she had been.

"Let's go inside and talk," Will suggested. Since they first met him two years ago, he had elected himself as the family's communication expert. He was "in touch with his emotions," as psychologists put it, and he was bent on getting the rest of the family in touch with theirs, too. Libby and Maggie were the easiest for him to deal with because they were the softest and most like him. Anne and her father were almost exactly alike, and they were equally as uncomfortable with matters of the heart. Kitty was somewhere in the middle, and could go either way depending on her mood.

Dobbie fell in the camp with Anne and her father, so it was no surprise when he rolled his eyes to Libby behind Will's back. It was a surprise when he took her hand, twined their fingers together, and wouldn't let go when she tried to escape.

"Don't," he said, and his tone told her it was useless to argue. Instead she sat stiffly and uncomfortably beside him on the couch, feeling visible and on display while Anne and Will detailed their journey home.

"We tried to get home in time for Libby's birthday yesterday," Anne explained and gave a pointed look to Will.

"Some day soon this woman is going to get me killed," Will said. "She almost got into a fist fight with the ticket agent at the airport. They actually called security on her and threatened to arrest her, but I talked them out of it."

"Sure, *that* you use your talking skills for, but a stubborn and rude ticketing agent you totally ignore," Anne returned.

"Annie, there was a hurricane. What did you want the poor woman to do?"

"If she was good at her job, she could have figured something out."

He shook his head. "So anyway, we arrive at the train station in town, and she tells me she's going to borrow a horse for us to ride out here on."

Everyone laughed at that. It was a bumpy and uncomfortable one hour car ride over dirt roads. A horse would not be a pleasant way to go.

"I literally had to pick her up like a football and clamp my hand over her mouth while I arranged for someone to drive us out here. And she's like this all the time. I am utterly exhausted." His words belied his actions, though, because he put his arms around her and gave her cheek and affectionate kiss.

Anne smiled and snuggled closer to him. Libby studied Dobbie out of the corner of his eye. Was it painful for him to see them this way? Was he picturing himself in Will's place? How could he not, she thought. Anne was a fireball. She was like a force of nature. Compared to her, Libby was as spineless and bland as a glass of luke-warm milk.

She stood and shook free of Dobbie. "You guys must be starved. I'll make you some food." Dobbie stood to follow, and she wanted to stamp her foot in consternation. She wanted to be alone. On the other hand, she didn't want to deny him an escape if he was hurting.

"What's wrong with you?" he hissed as soon as they were alone in the kitchen.

"Me? You're the one who's hurting."

"I am?" His surprise looked genuine.

"Aren't you?" she asked.

"No."

"Oh." Her eyes dropped to his chest. "But aren't you jealous of him?"

"Yes, I am," he admitted, and her heart sank. He used his index finger to tip her face to his. "He gets to be with his girl and live happily ever after, but you and I can't seem to get started."

"Oh."

He took her face in his hands, his thumb smoothing over her bottom lip. "Libby Chapman, some day soon you and I are going to have a serious talk, and you might be surprised by what you find out."

It was happening again. She was becoming mesmerized. "I might?"

He took a step closer, backing her against the wall until she was pinned against him. "Yes. And after we talk, I'm going to kiss you, and then kiss you again and again, and maybe again. We'll have to see how it goes."

"Oh." She blinked at him a few times, not sure what to say. Her hands rested on his chest, curling the soft fabric in her fists. "That sounds nice."

"Yes it does, and if your family doesn't stop interrupting these intimate moments between us, I'm going to let your goat out of his pen and force another campout."

"Don't you touch my goats, Shane Dobbins." She tried to say it fiercely, but it lost something when her fingers smoothed softly over his sculpted chest.

"I might actually die if this thing between us doesn't get some resolution soon. Do you think anyone has ever exploded from wanting to kiss someone so much?"

"We could ask Kitty to look it up for us."

"I'm pretty sure the answer is no," Kitty said from the doorway, and Dobbie and Libby jumped apart so abruptly she banged into the counter and had to lunge for a jam jar before it toppled to the ground. "Dad sent me in to see what's taking so long. I probably shouldn't tell him." With that she spun on her heel and headed back to the living room.

"Maybe we should get jobs in Siberia," Dobbie said as he helped her set out containers of food. "It's less crowded there."

"I don't think there are any ranches in Siberia," she said.

"That's because no one has ever tried. We could be pioneers. Think of the possibilities."

"We live in the middle of nowhere in Montana. We're already pioneers."

"And do you think of the possibilities?" he asked, scrutinizing her with a serious expression.

In truth she had thought of the possibilities here. She knew she could start different ventures that would bring in more money, like her goats. "Some," she admitted.

"I think we have more to talk about than either of us realizes," he said and bent to carry the loaded tray into the living room.

CHAPTER 22

The room Will had lived in during his summer on the ranch had been converted into her father's office, so Libby gave him her room and squeezed in with Kitty. Anne looked slightly hurt that she didn't stay with her, but she was nervous to be alone with Anne. She still felt like she was invading her territory somehow.

To her relief, Anne went out early the next morning, leaving Libby time to talk to Will. He smiled at her all through breakfast and hung around the kitchen after everyone else left.

"So Libby and Dobbie, how are we feeling about that?" he asked.

She sat across from him and dropped her forehead onto the table with a decided thump.

"What's up, Libby?"

"I'm so confused, Will. I care about Dobbie, but it's unexpected, and new, and scary, and a part of me still wants to go away and see what else is out there, and who else is out there."

"You know, sometimes what we want and what we think we need are the same thing, and we try to complicate it because it seems too easy," Will said. He was always saying things like that, like a riddle. It drove plain-speaking Anne crazy, but Libby liked the way it made her think things through.

"Do you think Dobbie and the ranch are the right choice for me?" she asked.

"I couldn't begin to tell you what is the right choice for you. All I'm telling you is that sometimes the answer that makes us happy is also the right decision."

"That only helps if I know what answer makes me happy." She stretched out her arm in front of her and laid her head on it.

"Are you happy when you're with Dobbie?" Will asked.

She thought of Dobbie, how he made her laugh, how she felt protected and safe whenever they were together, and how he needed her, too. Then she thought of kissing him, how wonderful it had been, and how much she wanted to do it again.

"Yes, I'm happy when I'm with Dobbie. I feel fulfilled when we're together, but I'm also restless and afraid if I stay here, I'll always wonder what else is out there."

"Poor, confused Libby," Will said. He reached out to grasp her hand.

Unfortunately Dobbie chose that moment to pause in the doorway and observe them, and then he quickly turned on his heel and fled the house.

Will squeezed her hand. "Take the advice of someone who deals with your sister on a daily basis: when someone's heart is as hard to get at as a prickly pear, it's better to go after him early and often."

"Thanks, Will." She squeezed his hand. they shared a smile and she went to find Dobbie.

He was in the barn brushing his sweaty horse. That meant he had stopped in the house to see her before tending to his horse. He was fastidious in the grooming of his horse, so she knew the fact he had put it off was an indicator of how much he had wanted to see her. He didn't stop what he was doing, and he didn't speak or acknowledge her presence in any way.

"You know Will's like a brother to me," she said gently.

"I was like a brother to you once," he said curtly and kept brushing.

"You've been a lot of things to me, Dobbie, but a brother has never been one of them."

That softened him somewhat. "You and he are a lot alike."

"So are you and Anne."

That did it. He threw the brush to the ground and advanced on her. She backed up against the wall, eyes wide. He picked her up by the upper arms until she was eye level with him.

"Now, you listen to me. I never felt for Anne the way I feel for you. The most meaningful conversation of our lives revolved around calving. Yes, I looked at engagement rings, but only because I didn't want him to take what I thought belonged to me, and I still feel that way. You'll notice I never bought one, and the more I think about it I'm not sure I ever would have. I don't want her. I want you, Libby, I want you so much." His tone and his hands softened, and now the weight of his body was pressing her against the wall.

She pressed her palms to his cheeks. "I don't want him. I don't want Marcus. I don't want anyone but you."

"But for how long?" he asked the anguishing question that hung like a barrier between them.

Hooves thundered nearby. Anne streaked into the barn and dismounted her horse without stopping it. She froze when she saw Dobbie and Libby in their intimate embrace, but Libby felt only a mild discomfort in her presence now, the same as she would for anyone who had caught them pressed together as they were. Somehow Dobbie's speech had given her release where her sister was concerned. He didn't love Anne; maybe he never had.

"Sorry," Anne said. "I would go, but I have to tend to my horse." She was as much a stickler for proper horse care as Dobbie was.

"I have to go back to the house anyway," Libby said. She gave Dobbie a feather soft kiss on the lips, and he closed his eyes as if he were in pain.

"Like a squirt gun on a forest fire," he said and let her go. "I'll fix up your horse, Anne. You girls go on together." He took the reins from Anne as then she and Libby started for the house.

"So, you and Dobbie," Anne laughed, and shook her head. "Will said this would happen."

"He did?" Libby asked, incredulous.

"When we left for school a couple of years ago, I was pretty upset about hurting Dobbie, but Will said Dobbie didn't love me. He said you and Dobbie had passionate chemistry, but you didn't know it yet."

Had Will really seen what was coming between her and Dobbie so long ago? Amazing. "Is it okay with you?" she asked tentatively.

"Okay?" Anne repeated. "Okay that my oldest friend and little sister are getting together? It's better than okay, it's the happiest news I've ever heard."

"But I don't know that it's happening for sure. There's still college in the fall."

"I don't blame you for wanting to get away and test your own wings, Lib, but because you're going away doesn't mean you can't be together. Lots of couples date long distance."

"I don't think Dobbie would go for that. I think he would feel insecure about me being so far away and near so many other men, and he might feel like he was holding me back."

"That sounds like him, the big dummy. Try not to worry about it. If it's meant to be, then it will work out."

"Are you turning into a romantic?" Libby asked.

"I'm afraid so," Anne said sadly. "But you try falling in love with the best guy in the world and still maintain a cynical attitude. It's impossible."

After supper everyone sat around talking while Libby knitted. She asked Anne and Will what it was like to live in the city, and by the way Dobbie tensed beside her, they all knew she was trying to picture herself there.

Will took the lead. "It's great. There's a store on every corner, and on Saturdays they bring in fresh produce."

"You only get fresh produce once a week?"

"Yes. In the summer, that is. In the winter it's less frequent, obviously."

Libby thought of her large and bountiful garden with a stab of remorse. "Doesn't anyone grow their own food?"

"Oh, no. The buildings are all so tall and close together that the sun can't filter through, and there's no grass."

"No sun and no grass?" Libby asked, aghast.

Anne smacked Will in the stomach. "There are parks, and they're beautiful, and some of them have community gardens."

"That's true," Will said, nodding his agreement. "You could have a couple of feet to grow things, if you're willing to pay a fee and don't mind when people steal your food."

"People steal your food?" Libby asked, her knitting forgotten in light of her sudden distress. The city was beginning to sound like a terrible place.

"Oh, people steal everything in the city, your food, your purse, your phone, your identity. Your life."

Anne stared at Will, perplexed. She had no idea why he was making it sound like they lived in a post-apocalyptic wasteland. "Will, I've lived in the city for two years, and I've never been mugged."

"Yes, but you're you," Will said, and everyone nodded their agreement. Anne was small, like Libby, but she exuded an air of "touch me and it will be the last thing you ever do."

Will went on to list major crime statistics for their city, and then he detailed a particularly heinous murder that was still unsolved. By the end of his story, Anne was frowning at him in confusion, Libby's hands were trembling on her knitting needles, and Dobbie was smiling happily. When no one was looking he gave Will a slight heads-up nod, and Will pretended to tip his hat in return.

CHAPTER 23

By the time Anne and Will left two days later, Dobbie had made peace with both of them. On the morning of their departure, he and Anne took a ride together, and when they returned, it was as if their old friendship was resurrected. While they were gone, Will and Libby amused themselves by imagining all the ways they were reconnecting.

"I bet she'll punch him in the shoulder," Libby said.

"Are you joking?" Will asked. "She only jilted him; shoulder punching is for when you do something really bad, like accidently poison his favorite bull. I think an impersonal nod will clear the air between them."

The downside to all of the couple bonding was that Dobbie and Libby had no alone time together, and after Will and Anne departed they were busy catching up on all the work they had missed during the visit.

The next week life was slowing down and returning to normal again when a huge rainstorm hit. It had been hot and dry for two weeks, so everything became muddy, and then muddier, and then turned into mud soup.

Libby met Dobbie at the door that night with her hands on her hips. "You look like an aborigine. I can only see the whites of your eyes."

He grinned at her and his teeth flashed. "Do you find aborigines attractive?"

"Not when they're about to track mud on floors I've spent two days scrubbing spotless."

"Libby, I'm wet, cold, exhausted and famished. I took off my boots and chaps, but that's as clean as I'm going to get."

"How does Dad always manage to stay clean while you get covered?" she asked.

"Because it's his ranch and he has the privilege of staying on his horse when a newborn calf gets stuck in the mud. Now move aside, please."

"Shower and change. I'll keep supper hot."

"Woman, you are testing my patience. Move aside."

She lifted her chin and crossed her arms over her chest. They stared each other down at the edge of the kitchen.

He bent his shoulder to her stomach, picked her up, and slung her over his back like a sack of potatoes. For good measure, he smacked her on the behind and set her down in the kitchen. That was when he realized he had indeed left a trail of mud from the door, and now her pretty pink dress was caked in it. Still, he was too proud to apologize and sat without a word.

Libby served supper, also without a word, and then served pie, to everyone except Dobbie. It was apple pie, his favorite, so the wound cut deep.

"Where's my pie?" he asked.

"Sorry, we're fresh out," she said.

He stood and barged from the house.

He had to shower twice to get all the dirt off, and when he entered the kitchen she was still on her hands and knees scrubbing mud.

"You're the only woman I know who scrubs the floor in a dress," he said. She raised her head and wrinkled her nose at him. He went forward, picked her up, and swallowed her in his embrace.

"I'm sorry. You know I get cranky when I'm hungry. I guess I was pretty dirty."

She slid her arms around his neck. "I shouldn't have tried to keep you from your supper." She reached to the counter behind him and presented him with a plate. "I saved you something." It was a huge slice of the apple pie. He looked at it, and then at her, and it was as if a bolt of sudden understanding hit him, knocking him senseless with the newfound knowledge. He opened his mouth, but no words came out.

"Are you okay?" she asked worriedly. She touched her fingertips lightly to his cheek.

"I.." he started. He heard movement in the other room and knew they were about to be interrupted again. He set the pie on the counter, took her hand, and practically dragged her from the house. They barely made it to the hidden spot on the porch before he turned and kissed her with all the passion and ferocity that had been building between them. He tangled his hands in her hair and pulled her impossibly closer while they kissed until they were both breathless and trembling. He knew he should release her, but he couldn't bring himself to do it. He kissed her until she was unable to support herself and leaned all her weight on him. At last he released her and rested his forehead on hers.

"You can't go, Libby. All this time we've been thinking we're all wrong for each other, but it finally hit me: we're perfect for each other. We're exactly what the other needs. I love you, I love you so much, Lib, and together we can make this ranch into something great. We can make *us* into something great." He kissed her again, and she melted into him.

Even as they kissed, though, she could feel the imaginary shackles of commitment snake around her legs. If she committed to Dobbie, she would be committing to the farm for life, and she wasn't sure she could do that yet.

She broke off the kiss and backed against the wall away from his embrace.

"What's wrong?" he asked.

"I got my letter today from school confirming my start date and sending me a list of supplies," she blurted. She had no idea how to tell him what was on her heart, so she said the first thing that came to mind.

Dobbie drew himself up, and his face closed off. "And you're choosing school over me. You're going away."

"I, I," she started, and then stopped, unsure of how to continue. "It doesn't have to be this way, Dobbie. We could be together while I'm at school. We could date long distance."

"That's not how I'm wired, Libby. I can't give you that. I can't be away from you and in a relationship together. It wouldn't work." He paused, giving her a chance to respond. When she didn't, a heavy sort of regret settled between them. "Keep your pie," he said stiffly, and then he walked away.

After that, the atmosphere between them was arctic. They didn't talk, they didn't touch, and they didn't look at each other. Everyone noticed the tension, but no one knew what had caused it, and no one knew how to fix it, so everyone kept silent.

Libby was heartbroken and more confused than ever. The fact that Dobbie loved her and freely admitted it threw her for an unexpected loop. Was he right? Did they belong together? Could they make it work? They had a strong attraction to each other, that was undeniable. But they were very different. Would those differences help them to work as a team or eventually make them enemies? Every time she leaned in his direction, she felt a tremor of fear and a pull toward the unknown. And she resented his stiff-necked attitude. Why did it have to be his way or nothing? Why couldn't he compromise? She was sure they could make a long distance relationship work if they tried. No doubt it would be difficult, but they could do it. Couldn't they? Or was he right and it would ruin all that was between them?

For the next few days, they tiptoed around each other. Each of them wanted to fix things between them, but neither knew how. And both of them were hurt, angry and unable to understand the other's viewpoint. Libby didn't understand why Dobbie was being so hard-nosed about his stance. Dobbie felt like Libby would be leaving him for greener pastures. After Anne's betrayal, trust came harder.

The next week, Libby entered the kitchen and interrupted a conversation between Dobbie and her father. They were never both home in the middle of the day, so she knew it was something dire.

"What is it?" she asked.

Neither man answered her, and she was filled with fear.

"What is it? Please tell me," she pled.

"The ranch is in trouble," Dobbie blurted. Matt shot him a quelling glare. "She deserves to know, Matt. It's her home, too."

"What do you mean by trouble? I thought the tourists were going to help."

"They did some," her father said. "But there's a new bank manager, an out-of-towner. He's making a bad name for himself by being a stickler for rules. He's called our note. I'm tapped out, and I won't have the money to pay it until the cattle auction in the fall. He says if we don't have it by the first of September he's going to take the ranch."

She hid her distress. It wouldn't do to become hysterical right now. "How much is needed?"

Both men looked at her in silence again.

"Would you tell Anne?" she asked Dobbie, and he smiled slightly.

"Thirteen thousand dollars, sweet," he said.

It was a grim and telling amount. If her father couldn't raise that small amount, then they really were in trouble. "I have ten thousand dollars in the bank. We'll use that," Libby volunteered.

"We're not using your money, Libby," her father said, using the tone that said he expected no further argument.

"Dad, as Dobbie pointed out, it's my ranch, too. Besides, I earned that money off the ranch from my jam and wool and what I sold to the tourists."

"You could probably sell snow cones to Eskimos, you know that, Lib?" Dobbie said with a fond smile.

"And then I'd sell them embroidered napkins to wipe their fingers," she added and he snorted a laugh.

"I appreciate that, honey, but that still leaves us three thousand short," her father said. She hated to see the lines of defeat settling into his features.

"The banker won't give you an extension for such a paltry amount?" she asked.

"He's a hard-nosed so and so," her father said. He didn't curse, and for him to call someone a so and so was akin to a nasty expletive of dislike.

"I might have an idea," she said. Dobbie and her father looked at her hopefully, another sign of how bad things really were. "Huckleberries."

"Huckleberries," they echoed in disbelieving unison.

"The tourists can't get enough huckleberries," she said. They still looked incredulous. "They sell for over thirty dollars a gallon," she added, and was satisfied when their jaws dropped. "We'll check into shipping them raw to the markets in Billings and I can make jam. I'll start a website and contact all of our campers to see if they want to buy some. They all bought cookbooks, and I included huckleberry recipes on the off chance I would get my hands on some berries. We're going to need every spare hand, though. I'm going to need two men to guard for bears and anyone you can spare to pick. Once the picking is done, I can handle it alone from there."

They had less than a month, and she wasn't sure they could pull it off. But if she had to, she would swallow her pride and borrow the remaining amount from Marcus. She didn't want to, though. She wanted to do it with her family all working together. She felt invigorated, more so than she had ever been. In a way, she felt like she had finally found what she was meant to do, and she set upon it with a vengeance.

That night she started a website with the help of one of Kitty's computer-savvy contacts. She advertised the items she had already made, along with her made-to-order cashmere sweaters. She set aside a large amount of wool and contacted a yarn store in Billings to buy the excess. They agreed, and that netted her a few hundred dollars. Next she called Mr. Smith and learned he had another three hundred dollars in jam money ready for her. He was also elated at the prospect of huckleberry jam and assured her he could sell as much as she could make, and for a dollar more per jar. Finally she asked him if he knew of anyone in need of eggs, and he directed her to a pie baker in the next county over. She thanked him and called the pie maker. She told the woman who answered they had a surplus of free-range eggs from their chickens, which they did, and the woman offered to buy ten dozen for thirty dollars. Libby realized that would hardly cover the cost to deliver them, so she asked if the woman was in need of huckleberries, and the woman practically swooned from excitement. She agreed to pay above market price if they could be delivered on the day they were picked.

Libby hung up the phone, exhausted but happy. She had made almost a thousand dollars, and it was only the first day.

CHAPTER 24

The cattle enterprise came to a standstill as huckleberry picking commenced. Libby would soon regret her arrogance from the night before. It was hot, and the berries were small and hard to reach because of the brambles. The flies and mosquitoes were out in force, and twice Dobbie and Rook had to fire warning shots to scare away approaching grizzlies. In addition to that, there was the logistical problem of getting pickers and equipment to the berry patch, and then getting the berries safely out. The truck couldn't reach the berries, and the berries couldn't be left alone on the truck because of the bears. Libby was hot, tired, and irritable, and she wished she had never heard of huckleberries. It wasn't noon yet, and even Maggie complained, which was such a surprise that everyone stopped what they were doing and turned to look at her.

Still, when Dobbie returned after delivering a truckload of berries to the ranch he picked Libby up, twirled her in a circle, and set her down with a kiss on the cheek. "I'm proud of my pretty girl," he whispered softly in her ear.

Suddenly the day didn't seem so bad, and she began picking with renewed vigor.

They picked from sunup until sundown, and then Libby had to

make supper and start on the jam. Thankfully it was a light jam night because one cowhand had been dispatched to the pie lady while another had taken berries to the market in Billings. As it was, it was well after midnight when she went to bed, and she had to be up at five the next morning.

Every day became the same routine of picking all day, fixing supper, and making jam. Libby kept putting one foot in front of the other in the hope that everything would turn out all right.

"You look exhausted, sweet," Dobbie said. Libby turned to see him standing in the doorway of the kitchen. She wondered how long he'd been watching her unnoticed.

"So do you," she said. She turned to stir her jam, but also to avoid looking at him. They had barely talked lately, and she missed him with a yearning ache. She was afraid if he looked too closely, he would see the raw longing for him in her gaze.

He came to stand close behind her and raised a hand to massage her neck where it met her shoulders, as if he knew it was the precise spot that ached. "What can I do to help, baby girl?" He spoke softly because the rest of the house was already asleep.

"This is a good start," she said. She leaned toward him and pressed her back against his chest, sliding her eyes closed, resting with assurance that Dobbie had her covered, if only for a moment.

He pushed her hair aside and pressed a light kiss to her neck. "I hate to see you working this hard."

"I'm not working any harder than you," she said breathlessly. He was making it hard to focus on her task.

"I'm a man. Men are supposed to work hard. Ladies aren't." His thumb slid along the tender spot he'd just kissed.

"Ladies do whatever is necessary to protect their homes and their families." She tilted her head farther in the hopes he would kiss her again, but he didn't cooperate.

"Is that jam going to burn?"

Her eyes popped open and looked at the jam, which was boiling too hard. She jumped to attention, turned down the heat, and started to ladle the jam into the prepared jars.

"What can I do?" he asked again. "There must be something."

She assigned him the task of wiping the tops of the jars and securing the lids before she put them back in the water bath to boil. The time flew with him standing beside her, and it was over all too quickly. They didn't talk while they worked. He started to leave, but she held him back.

As they worked quietly side by side a memory surfaced, and she couldn't push away the feeling it brought with it. Her mother died when she was ten. Dobbie still lived at home with his parents then. Almost immediately after the funeral, Libby took over the household duties. Dobbie came to the door one day and knocked. When Libby opened it, he presented her with a bouquet of flowers.

"Anne's not home," she had said, taking the wilted little bouquet in hands that already felt calloused from scrubbing.

"They're not for Anne," Dobbie had said with something like shyness, his eyes on his boots. "They're for you." She had blinked at him in mute surprise, and then he was gone.

"Why did you bring me the flowers?" she asked aloud. "When my mom died, why did you bring me flowers and not Anne?"

"Because Anne would have taken the flowers and smacked me upside the head with them," he said. "And I was out walking, saw the flowers, and thought of you. I knew they would make you feel better." He paused. "I always think of you when I see wildflowers, Libby. I always have, and I always will." He didn't wait to see her reaction to his words before he turned and walked out the door.

She stared at the spot he vacated. Dobbie had known flowers would make her feel better, even back when they were children. He knew how to fix her when she was hurting, when she was scared, when she was upset, when she was angry. He knew in the same way she knew what he needed when he was feeling low. Could it be he was right, that they were meant for each other after all?

For the next three weeks, the entire ranch kept up the same furious pace, and for the first time in anyone's memory the laundry went undone, and dust bunnies roamed the hallways. Libby didn't care, though; she couldn't. All of her energy went into picking and boiling and watching the ever-growing pile of money. Sometimes Dobbie came at night to help her with canning, and sometimes he didn't. He was functioning under his own strain trying to keep up with helping her pick and all of his regular ranch duties. On the nights he did help her can, he worked in silence and didn't attempt any more physical advances. But still his presence was a comfort. For better or worse, they were in this together. Each of them understood the burden they were under, and each of them tried their best to ease some of the load for the other.

Finally the huckleberry patch was picked dry, the jam was all sold, and they were a hundred dollars short. With a shout, Maggie remembered her father's giant coin jar in the back of his closet.

Libby made popcorn and cookies, and they spent the night before the deadline counting and rolling coins. When it was all said and done, they were fifty dollars over their goal.

They all cheered and danced around the kitchen, even Matt who was usually stoic.

"You did it, Lib," Dobbie whispered.

"*We* did it," she returned.

Overjoyed and not caring who saw, he swept her up and kissed her breathless in front of everyone. This time he was the one who broke it off, and Libby was left yearning for more as he went to see to the animals.

Over the next couple of weeks, they circled each other warily. Libby felt like they were testing the waters with each other and dipping their toes in before yanking them quickly back out. Dobbie started staying after supper again to help her with the cleanup, and they talked, really talked, about everything on their minds. Libby told him her plans and dreams for the ranch, and he listened intently and openly. He made suggestions of his own, and one night they sat at the kitchen table sketching out their ideas.

"I think we should move your goats over here," he said. He took the pencil from her and leaned over her to sketch a new pen for the goats. "If you add another male and female this fall, you could have four new kids in the spring. That's a good start for a small herd."

He continued to sketch while she watched him. He was absorbed in his work and didn't notice her inspection. He did notice when she touched her fingertips to his face and traced them lovingly over his cheek. He froze and looked at her, his face a centimeter from hers.

She turned so she was fully facing him and brought her other hand to his face. She studied the contours of his face with her fingertips, and he closed his eyes. When she kissed him lightly on the lips, he didn't respond; he remained frozen, but he didn't pull away. She kissed him gently until he began to respond, and then they heard someone heading toward the kitchen.

"Siberia," she muttered. He chuckled and pulled away to stand upright.

Kitty entered the kitchen, returned her glass to the sink, and slipped away without a word. Dobbie resumed his seat at the table beside Libby and they studied the drawing in front of them.

"What is this?" she asked, tapping the building he had drawn.

"A house," he said, not taking his eyes off the paper.

"A house?" she repeated.

"It's not practical to think of living here with your dad forever. One of us is going to be married someday, and we've already seen how little privacy there is. Imagine being a newlywed here." He shuddered.

She shuddered, too, but for another reason. The thought of Dobbie living in the phantom house he had drawn, married to another woman, was painful. But she didn't know how to broach the subject, so she didn't.

They talked about everything but their relationship. Libby knew they couldn't put it off much longer, but she was enjoying the prolonged peace between them and didn't want to do anything that might disturb it.

When they finished the dishes each night after that, they went to sit in the other room with the rest of the family. At first they sat side by side without touching, but as the night progressed, they inched toward each other until they were pressed tightly together. On the third night of sitting next to each other, Dobbie took her hand and Libby rested her head on his shoulder. The next night the same thing happened, except he added a gentle goodnight kiss when it was time to say goodbye.

The next night started out with the same sort of promise, and then Kitty carried a large box into the room.

"More books, Kitty?" Dobbie asked. He had coaxed Libby to take her hair out of its confines and was currently running his fingers through it. "I can't believe there are any you haven't read yet."

"I thought they were mine, but they're not. They're Libby's." She opened the box and pulled out a college textbook.

Dobbie froze and sat up straight, untangling his hands from her hair. He looked like he had been sucker punched. "You're still going," he said hoarsely. "And I'm the world's biggest idiot. Again." He didn't give her the chance to respond before he stood and fled the house.

"Aren't you going to go after him?" Kitty asked.

"I'll let him cool off, and I'll talk to him in the morning," Libby replied. Will's warning to go after him early and often flashed in her mind, but she ignored it. She was peeved Dobbie had stormed out in such an irrational rage. And, if she was being honest, she had to admit there was a little part of her that was still angry over his unbending attitude. Why did it have to be his way or the highway?

Later she would regret letting him go.

CHAPTER 25

"He's gone," Maggie yelled as she burst into the kitchen the next morning.

"What are you talking about?" Libby asked, although she already knew the answer.

"Rook said his stuff was cleared out when he woke up this morning," Maggie said, and her eyes swam with tears. "It's like the last time."

No, it wasn't. It couldn't be because Libby wouldn't allow it. What would she do if he was really gone? She might never find him again. Panic started to blot out rational thought, but she pushed it away. She had to think. He couldn't take the truck or his horse because both belonged to her father. He would have to go on foot; it was the same way he left last time. He wouldn't have gone at night, which meant he couldn't have been gone long because the sun had barely risen.

"Maggie, can I borrow your pony?" Libby asked.

Maggie sniffed and looked at Libby in confusion. She didn't usually ride for pleasure. "Sure, but why…" Realization began to dawn and she began to smile. "She's already saddled. I was going to ask him if I could ride with him today."

Libby kissed her cheek. "Maggie, you're the best." She sprinted past her.

"Aren't you going to change?" Maggie called.

"No time," Libby yelled. It wasn't easy to mount a horse while wearing heels and a dress, but she did it and took off at a furious pace. He couldn't have gotten far, she reassured herself. She would find him; she had to.

The beauty of the country was that there was only one road in or out of town, so eventually she would find him, as long as he hadn't gotten a ride with someone. As she reached the end of their long lane, she saw him getting ready to hit the road. He didn't look back when he heard her approach, but he did hunch his shoulders as if preparing for a blow. He probably thought it was her father or Rook. Well, if a blow was what he wanted, then a blow was what he would get.

She kicked off her shoes and readied herself in the saddle. When she got close enough she pounced, knocking him to the ground.

"Libby," he exclaimed as he caught her. He took her full weight and made a protective cage around her with his arms as they hit the ground and rolled, finally landing with her on top. "Are you crazy? You could have been hurt. What are you doing?"

"I could ask you the same thing," she said. "What are you doing?"

"I'm leaving," he said defensively.

"You promised you wouldn't again," she reminded him.

"As long as I was wanted."

"Who said you're not wanted, you stubborn mule-headed cowboy?" They were shouting now, which was unnecessary because she still had him pinned to the ground and their faces were nose to nose.

"You did," he yelled. "You're leaving, too. I won't stay and wait for you, only to watch you come home with some city slicker who could never deserve you."

"You've got it all figured out, don't you?" she shouted.

"I'm smart that way," he raged.

"You don't know everything. You only think you do."

"Tell me what I don't know," he demanded. "I dare you."

"I'm not leaving, so there."

"You're…not…leaving," he said it like he was trying to fit together a puzzle, but was missing the last piece.

She gathered his shirt in her hands and tried to give him a shake, but of course it was like shaking granite. Drat him and his muscles. "It's the middle of September, Dobbie. Classes started three weeks ago. I'm starting an online degree next quarter, that's what the books were for."

He blinked up at her and then slowly, ever so tentatively, reached up to touch her hair, which despite the rough ride and flying leap, remained obediently in its twist. "But why? Why did you decide to stay?"

"Remember how you told me you had to go away before you realized this was your home?"

"Yes," the remembrance of missing her sliced through him, making the words a painful whisper.

"I had to face losing my home to realize how much it meant to me. I can't lose the ranch; I love it here. It's a part of me, and I need it. Plus, it was fun to boss everyone around with the huckleberries, like running my own corporation. I can get my degree, stay here, and be an entrepreneur. I want to start implementing some of the things we've been talking about."

"So that's the only reason you stayed?" he asked.

"Yes, of course, it's all about the ranch." She tried to shake him again. "Oh, and also because I love, love, love you, and the thought of being without you even for a day scares me more than grizzlies."

"You…love…me." He said it in the same puzzled tone.

"Sweetheart, I galloped here on a horse in a dress and heels and took a flying leap at your head. I love you, I'm staying, and we're going to be together forever and ever. Try and keep up, Dobbie."

He grinned at her and clutched her to him. "You know, it's not very ladylike to ride in a dress and fling yourself at a gentleman, Miss Chapman."

"Hush up and kiss me, Mr. Dobbins."

"Try and keep up," he said, and then he kissed her.

It was a long time later when they rode back to the house. For a brief moment both of them felt like they were on holiday, but as they approached the house reality started to sink back in.

"There's always so much to do," Libby said. "Most of the time I don't mind, but every once in a while I want to be a kid and do nothing." They reached the barn, and he helped her dismount from the pony.

"Let's," he said. "One day of fun out of a thousand days of work isn't going to dismantle the universe. We'll declare today a holiday and spend the day together doing absolutely nothing." He pulled the saddle off the pony and held it in both hands.

She looked at him, debating. A part of her felt guilty for even thinking of shirking her duties for the day.

"Don't tell me you're going to argue with me," he said. "We both know how that will end."

That did it. While his hands were full with the saddle she stood on her toes, whipped his hat off his head, and ran into the barn with it, giggling.

He hung the saddle carefully on its peg. When he turned to search the barn, she was nowhere in sight. A flash of yellow caught the corner of his vision, and he looked up to see the hem of her dress dangling from the edge of the hayloft. He smiled to himself and ascended the ladder, and his smile widened when he saw she was completely buried in the hay.

"I hope you aren't lying on that rat's nest I saw last week," he said.

She squealed and began furiously trying to dig her way out of the hay. He realized he didn't actually want her to leave yet.

"Kidding," he said. "I'll take my hat now." He held out his hand for it.

She grinned. "Come and get it, cowboy."

"I was hoping you would say that." He plopped down beside her and reached for her when they heard voices below.

"Siberia," they mouthed together, but he kissed her anyway, softly and sweetly. When the voices grew more distinct, they broke apart and scooted to the edge of the loft to spy on whoever was below.

Libby put her hand over her mouth to suppress a giggle. She felt like a naughty little girl—something she hadn't been in a long, long time.

Kitty was in the barn, which was unusual, and she was talking to Mathew Henshaw. Libby could only make out every other word, but it sounded as if they were talking about something mundane, like the weather.

"I'm going to find Maggie now," Mathew said. He tipped his hat politely to Kitty and left the barn. She stared after him for a moment and turned to face the interior of the barn. When she did, Libby caught her breath. There was a sad, wistful look on her face, and she swiped a few tears. She saddled Anne's horse and took off toward the north pasture.

Dobbie and Libby scooted away from the edge and rolled onto their backs, linking arms as they stared up at the rafters.

"What do you suppose that's about?" Dobbie asked.

"I don't know."

"You don't think Kitty would be foolish enough to have a crush on Mathew, do you?" he asked. "Everyone knows it's Maggie he wants."

"I don't know," Libby said again, sounding disturbed. She hated to think of her little sister hurting, and she hated even more the thought of what might happen if Mathew Henshaw came between Maggie and Kitty.

"Libby," Dobbie said seriously. "You're not allowed to be sad or serious on our day off. It's the law."

She smiled, then suppressed it and tried to sound despondent again. "What happens if I break the law?"

"Then I'll have to punish you most severely." The way he said it and sat up to lean over her made her spine start to tingle.

"Get ready, because I'm very, very, *very* sad," and, smiling, she tilted her face up to be kissed.

*T*hank you for reading *One Classy Cowgirl,* Book 2 in the Queens of Montana series. For more books, please check out my website at www.vanessagraybartal.com